THE SUMMER ULTIMATUM

PART OF THE SUMMERS IN SEASIDE SERIES

AMANDA SHELLEY

Visit my website at
www.amandashelley.com

CONNECT WITH AMANDA SHELLEY

Want to be the first to know about upcoming sales and new releases? Make sure you sign up for my newsletter as well as connect with me on social media and your favorite retail store.

Website:
www.amandashelley.com
Newsletter:
https://geni.us/AmandaShelleyNL
Facebook:
https://www.facebook.com/authoramandashelley/
Instagram:
https://www.instagram.com/authoramandashelley/
Reader's Group:
https://www.facebook.com/groups/AmandasArmyofReaders/
Tik Tok:
https://www.tiktok.com/@authoramandashelley
Amazon:
https://www.amazon.com/author/amandashelley
Goodreads:
https://www.goodreads.com/author/show/19713563.Aman
da_Shelley
Book Bub:
https://www.bookbub.com/profile/amanda-shelley

ABOUT THE BOOK

Watching my sister fall in love last summer gave me something I hadn't expected—hope. It gave me hope that there might be someone out there for me and hope that I might get past my misguided fears and finally let someone in.

With my help, Ryan's planning the most epic proposal. I just have to get the know-it-all musician I work with to fall in line to make it work.

Jax is wicked smart, extremely talented, and sexy as sin. But he can't see the forest for the trees when it comes to his potential. He'd rather keep playing in dive bars along the coast than take a real shot at success.

When the Seaside festival has a music competition, I present Jax with an ultimatum that will either make or break both our careers.

I've laid it all on the line, but can he?

Chapter 1
Sloane

"Quick, grab that high-top table over there," my sister Lanie urges as we enter the crowded club.

Pointing to the table in question, the bright neon X marked on my hand illuminates like a beacon, signaling the fact I'm still a minor in these black lights. It doesn't bother me though; I've got better things to do than drink. "This one?"

Nodding, she shouts above the music, "It's got the best view of the stage!"

Like the older sister she is, Lanie's always looking out for me. She knows how much I have riding on this internship. If I crush it, I'll be hired on permanently for my dream job. If I crash and burn, I'll never get a job in the entertainment industry. Yeah, I'm likely exaggerating, but it feels this way. The pressure is on.

Once we're seated, I lean in and ask, "When will Ryan get here?"

Ryan is Lanie's boyfriend. They met unexpectedly when she came to open Nana's house for the summer last year.

Despite the plan Nana put into place before she passed, I firmly believe Ryan is perfect for Lanie.

Looking at her phone, she grins like a fool. "He just texted to say he's running by his place to change, then he'll be here."

"Girl, you've got it bad," I tease, like any younger sister should. If my hunch is right, I have a feeling we'll finally be getting that boy in our family Dad has always hoped for. That guy is head over heels in love with my sister, and now that they've both graduated, I'm certain it will be only a matter of time before he pops the question.

Wistfully, Lanie sighs. "I can only hope one day, you'll find someone like Ryan."

"Uh, no thanks. I've got plans—and they don't include a man in my future."

I've worked my ass off to be the top of my class and even manage to surprise everyone by graduating early this spring. I have the internship of a lifetime lined up, and I'm focusing my energy on that.

I swear, Lanie's just as bad as Mom with her pointed looks. "You just wait, Sloane. You're gonna meet some guy who will completely knock you on your ass, and you'll be so stupid in love, you won't know what hit ya..." With a shit-eating grin, she smirks proudly. "And I'm here for it."

"Yeah. I don't think so. Don't get me wrong, I love that you've found the love of your life, but it's not in the cards for me for at least another few years."

"Oh, Sloaney..." She shakes her head as a knowing smirk slides into place. "You and your five-year plan."

"Hush." I swat at her, as the first band for open mic night steps up to the stage. "I need to pay attention." Pulling out the notebook I keep in my purse, I quickly jot down the band's name and my first impressions.

The lead singer steps up to the mic, introduces themselves,

then starts into a song I don't recognize. It's great they're playing their own songs, but they don't quite have the sound I'm looking for. They aren't bad, but nothing makes them stand out either. After a few songs, a new artist takes their place. Unfortunately, it's more of the same. They sound great for tonight's crowd, but there's nothing worth writing home about.

From the corner of my eye, I see my sister light up like a tree on Christmas as she spots something across the room. Obviously, Ryan's arrived. Nothing makes my sister look this happy, like him.

She's on her feet, embracing him the moment he arrives at our table. I know for a fact she saw him only this morning, as he left for work from our place. However, the two of them act like they've been apart for ten years, rather than ten hours.

I'll admit, I'm jealous—but not in the way most would think. I'm envious of her ability to open up and actually let him in. Someday, I want a man to look at me the way Ryan looks at Lanie. One who gets her so completely and pushes her to follow her dreams. But I'm not in any hurry. I've got plenty to focus on at the moment.

When they break apart, Ryan leans in to give me a side hug. "Hey, Sloane. You look great tonight. Thanks for suggesting we join you."

"No problem. I'm hoping to catch some local talent worthy of pitching to my boss."

Just as the words leave my mouth, a new musician comes to center stage with only a guitar and sits on the stool that's been provided for him. He's about my age and reminds me a bit like the comedian Matt Rife, with his predominant cheekbones, tousled hair, and gorgeous smile. Though he has a bit more scruff around his chiseled jaw, and it looks good on him. He's wearing worn jeans and a well-fitted black t-shirt and looks the part of a musician as he runs a hand through his hair before reaching for the mic.

Unlike the others who've performed before him, he's a bit raw. I can sense his nerves as he fumbles with the mic to adjust it before speaking. "Hi. I'm Jax Cartwright." The crowd cheers like they have for the other performers and when they settle down, he continues, "Some of you might remember me, but performing like this is a first tonight. I'm gonna play a few covers, along with one of my own. I hope y'all will enjoy this." He keeps it simple and to the point, but as he strums his guitar, checking if it's in tune, there's something about him that holds my attention.

Ryan leans in and says, "I went to school with this guy. He's a year younger than me. I never knew he could play."

The moment Jax strums the chords to Ed Sheeran's song, "Thinking Out Loud," Lanie squeals, jumping to her feet. "Ohmigod, I love this song! Dance with me, Ryan."

Ryan must agree because the next thing I know, I'm sitting alone at the table, completely mesmerized by Jax. His acoustic version of this song is on point. Before he can get to the chorus, I pull out my phone to capture his brilliance. The hairs on my skin stand to full attention as goose bumps erupt along my spine and up my arms as I watch him sing about falling in love. His timing and pitch are perfection, as his voice fills the room. By the time this song ends, I'm dying to know what else he's got in him.

Thankfully, Jax doesn't disappoint.

As the song ends, his sexy voice announces, "I'm gonna switch things up and play a personal favorite. This is the first song I ever learned to play. Hope you enjoy *my* version of 'American Pie.'"

I never would've picked this song, but the crowd goes wild as he hits the chorus, and they enthusiastically join him in his lyrics. Again, I've had my camera rolling from the beginning. It may originally be Don McLean's, but Jax quickly makes it his own. His ability to draw in a crowd is infectious. His raw talent holds everyone's interest.

By the time he launches into his own song, he's got the crowd hook, line, and sinker. They clap along enthusiastically. When he reaches the chorus for a second time, the audience joins in. The moment he finishes, I'm frantically sending all three videos to my boss with the following email:

Tara,
You HAVE to listen to Jax Cartwright. I think I've found our next local contestant for the showcase.
Let me know what you think,
Sloane

The moment Jax ends his set and leaves the stage, he makes a bee-line for the exit. I know within every fiber of my being, if I don't connect with him right this minute, I'll miss my chance.

Without a word to my sister or Ryan, I hop up from the table and hightail it across the room. Just as he exits the building, I call out, "Hey, Jax, wait up."

Chapter 2
Jax

My nerves are buzzing as I walk out the door. I just performed for the first time in front of a live audience, in my hometown of all places, and I'm dying to get out of here before anyone I know can stop me. I've never played locally. Playing in public was something I picked up my freshman year of college. I mostly played in the dorms or in small crowds. Tonight was about my promise to Dad—and now that it's done, I'm heading home.

I've just made it out the door when an unrecognizable female voice calls from behind me, "Hey, Jax, wait up."

At first, I'm tempted to pretend I didn't hear it and keep walking, but when she mentions, "I'm with Smashing Waves Records. Can I have a moment of your time?" it stops me in my tracks.

Why would someone from a studio want to talk with me?

When I turn around, I'm met with piercing hazel eyes. They belong to a girl about my age, with dark wavy hair and dressed far more professional than most in this coastal town. She's wearing a black skirt, with a fuchsia-pink blouse. It fits her perfectly, but she looks like she just came from the office, rather than someone who hangs out in a club. Before I can further assess her, she quickly thrusts her hand in my direction, officially introducing herself.

"Hi, I'm Sloane Lancaster from Smashing Waves Records Studio. I know you're busy, as you're rushing out of here, but do you think we could set up a time to talk in the next day or so?"

So much is in that introduction, I'm not even sure where to begin. But curiosity gets the better of me, so I ask, "What exactly do you want to talk about?"

Without hesitation, she smiles and says, "Your music, of course. You played one hell of a set and if you've got some time, I'd love nothing more than to set up a meeting to see what else you can do." Reaching out, she hands me a business card. "My number is on the back. I'd really like to talk with you."

Her confidence is sexy, but I'm so caught off guard by her offer, I'm sure I come off like an ass when I ask, "Why?"

Blinking a few times as if she can't comprehend my question, she inhales a deep breath before straightening her shoulders and repeating herself. "Like I said, I'm interested in your music. I think you've got an amazing voice, and your vibe on stage is just what we're looking for."

"I'm pretty sure you've got the wrong guy," I dismissively say. "This was a one-off—not my usual thing."

The phone in her other hand buzzes with an incoming message. She briefly glances at it but returns her attention to me. "Look, I won't take much of your time. But can you at least let me buy you dinner so we can discuss this further?"

Again, I'm both intrigued and confused by her persistence. "Uh, I work most nights this summer."

"How about lunch?" She must read something on my face because she quickly adds, "You gotta eat sometime. We can meet for breakfast or just coffee. Just text me when you're available, and we can set something up."

Sloane certainly isn't backing down. She's got a way about her that's assertive, but not at all bitchy or controlling. Her tenacity sparks my interest and makes me wonder what she's really like. I've never considered pursuing a career in music, but I'd certainly be interested in more time with her.

What's the worst that could happen? I spend time with a beautiful girl, and I turn her offer down? Seems like a no-brainer to me.

Not wanting to show my cards entirely, I suggest, "Meet me at Whitman's tomorrow at eight-thirty. The local morning rush should be gone, and the tourists won't be out of bed just yet. It should give us a chance to get a table where we can discuss things."

Nodding once, she grins. "I'll be there. I'd better get back in to watch the remaining sets tonight. My sister is probably wondering where I went. Thanks again for agreeing to meet with me."

She's here with her sister? That's interesting. Does that mean she's a local? Or is she only here on vacation? I think I remember seeing Smashing Waves Studio as one of the major companies sponsoring the music festival this summer, but they're based somewhere in California or something. I'm certain I've never seen her before—but as I put my truck into drive and pull out of the parking lot, all thoughts swirling through my brain are on her.

BETWEEN PLAYING on stage for the first time and my conversation with Sloane Lancaster, I was wound up most of the night. Even though I'd pulled a double, working the morning and lunch rush at the restaurant yesterday before my performance, and my body was exhausted, I couldn't sleep for shit last night.

Wanting to guarantee a table at the café, I arrive thirty minutes early, only to find Sloane typing away at her laptop in the back corner of the restaurant. When the hostess asks if I want a table for one, I point to Sloane. "My party has already arrived."

Sloane is so entranced in her work she doesn't even notice my approach. Today, she's wearing another flowy blue blouse, and her long hair is tied in a knot at the base of her neck. On her nose is a pair of dark-rimmed glasses, and serious Sloane is even sexier than last night.

When I reach her table, I stand for a few moments before clearing my throat to get her attention.

Startled, her body jerks slightly before turning her beautiful hazel eyes on mine. "Oh, I didn't expect you to be this early." Reaching for her coffee cup, she moves it aside and quickly puts her laptop on the seat beside her.

Sliding into the booth across from her, I ask, "Are you always this early to meetings?"

"Dad was Air Force, and I've been engrained since I could tell time that if you show up on time—you're late. Besides, I was already up and didn't want to wake my sisters."

The waitress arrives and refills Sloane's cup with coffee. When I push mine toward her, she fills it to the brim. With a cheery smile, she states, "I'll give you some time to look at the menu. Be back in a few."

As soon as she leaves, I ask, "Are you staying at a local hotel?"

"No, we're staying at Nana's—Uh, I guess it's our house... now that she's gone."

"So..." I draw out, trying to piece the puzzle together.

Before I can censor my thoughts, I blurt out, "You live around here?"

"Well, I have most summers since I was a kid. But like I said, my dad was in the Air Force, so we didn't live near here. Seaside was Nana's home and the one place we always return to. Even now that she's gone, it's still where we feel most at home."

Before taking another sip of coffee, I ask, "Is your entire family here for the summer?"

"No, only my sisters and me. Mom's a traveling nurse, and Dad's stationed at Lewis-McChord. But enough about me. We're supposed to be talking about you."

I knew it would just be a matter of time before she turned the table, but I'd much rather talk about her. Sighing heavily, I admit, "Trust me, you're way more interesting."

Chapter 3
Sloane

I'll admit I'm impressed he showed up so early for our meeting. You can tell a lot about a person who's punctual. This tells me I might not have pegged him right. Most musicians are rarely early; rather, they're egotistical and try pitching themselves to me the moment they learn my role in the company. Jax, surprisingly, is quite the opposite. He seems more interested in getting to know me than focusing on his career.

As the regional talent coordinator at Smashing Waves Records, I'm more than used to contending with the talent and their egos. But something's different with Jax. Sure, he's confident, but I'm not sensing his ego is out of check in the slightest. In fact, he's quite humble.

Needing to see if my gut instinct is right, I choose to take the lead from him and not talk about his music just yet. "You said last night that you're from Seaside. My sister's boyfriend mentioned you being in school with him. Have you always lived here?"

His brows knit together for the briefest of moments, then he asks, "Who's your sister's boyfriend?"

"Ryan Murdock. He and Lanie met last summer when Nana hired his family's company to renovate our house."

"Ryan's a great guy. He's been away at college for a while. I wasn't aware he was back in town. He still working with his dad?"

"Yeah, he and Lanie just graduated a few weeks ago. He's working with his dad's company, and she was just hired on at the middle school here in town. For the first time ever, she'll live here year-round."

"What about you? Do you live here year-round?"

"For now, I'm doing an internship with Smashing Waves Records. It's a huge opportunity, with the possibility of a full-time position if everything pans out. They've got offices in both Portland and LA as well as team members following the talent, so I'm not sure where I'll land."

Leaning forward to rest his arms on the edge of the table, he asks, "Does this mean you're here for the rest of the summer?"

Reel it in, Sloane. This isn't about you. Switch our focus to him. Tara's dying to get him to try out for the competition. Like me, she thinks he has what it takes.

"Yeah. I'm here through the end of July at least. Like I said, I'm not sure where I'll end up. But tell me, what got you into playing music like that last night?"

A slow smile spreads across his lips as he looks to his hands around his coffee mug. "I've been playing for the last couple of years."

"Do you play any other instruments?"

"Can I?" He pulls his lower lip under his teeth, then admits, "Yeah. I suppose. Mom started me with piano when I was younger. But I can also play bass and drums, besides lead guitar. But I wouldn't say I'm proficient enough to do much more than write music for songs on all of them."

Jax's modesty is refreshing. But after hearing his song last night, I'm curious. "Do you write most of your own music?"

Shrugging, he admits, "I've written quite a bit. But I also can cover quite a few crowd favorites."

Pulling up my calendar on my phone so I can get him onto my schedule, I eagerly ask, "When's your next gig? I'd love to check out more of your songs in another performance."

Instead of answering, Jax is suddenly extremely interested in his coffee cup.

As if on cue, our bubbly waitress uses this lull in conversation to take our orders. In a matter of minutes, we've ordered, and she leaves as quickly as she appeared.

When she disappears, I find Jax running one of his long fingers around the rim of his coffee mug. His lower lip is tucked under his teeth, and he looks as if he's holding something back. If I hadn't been looking, I might've missed it. He suddenly shakes his head and meets my gaze. "Look, I know your time is valuable, and I most certainly don't want to waste it. The truth is, I took this meeting because I found you intriguing. But I think you've got the wrong guy. Last night was my first performance—ever on stage with a crowd like that."

I blink in confusion as I sputter in disbelief. "Are you... kidding me? You've never performed on stage before... and you walked up there and slayed it. I knew your talent was raw, but you had me completely fooled."

Slowly, he swallows. "Like I said, I think you've got the wrong guy."

There's no way he could perform to that caliber and have this be one of his first performances. The man's got talent coming out his ears. Why the hell hasn't he been using it?

"Or I've just met my perfect match," I challenge. Thoughts of endless possibilities flow through my mind like a hurricane. If I have it my way, Jax won't know what hit him.

He raises a brow of his own in challenge. "And how am I your perfect match?"

Leaning back in the booth, he crosses his arms over his broad chest, staring me down. Before I can process all that needs to be done, he smirks. "I know we just met yesterday, but I can clearly see your brain at work and frankly, I'm almost scared to know what's swirling around in that head of yours."

"Oh, I'm only just beginning, trust me." I smirk at his apprehension. "Before I get too far ahead of myself, tell me, did you like performing last night?"

Jax takes a long breath and exhales slowly. "After I got past my nerves. I guess I did. But it's not like I have any plans to do it again."

Placing a palm on the table, I corner him. "When's your next night off?"

Cocking his head to the side as if he's trying to figure me out, he blurts out, "Tomorrow night, why?"

"What would you say if I told you I could book you a gig? The place my sister works at is looking for someone to draw in a Monday-night crowd. They don't have a big stage, but it would be perfect for an act like yours. Do you think you have material to perform for an hour or two?"

The moment my words are out, he snarks out, "Are you suddenly a talent agent, too?"

"Nope. Not at all. But I think you have what it takes. I'd love to watch you play and get some clips to promote you on social media. I'm certain they'll eat you up."

Ignoring my compliment, he narrows his eyes at me. "Where is this place exactly?"

"Pop's Hops." Lanie's working there one more summer until she starts teaching this fall. "Have you heard of the place?" It's a bar, but they've recently renovated and have an outside stage. I'll have to stay out of the bar itself, but I'll be able to watch Jax perform from a table outside.

"Sloane," he says in a tone that makes my stomach flutter way more than it should. "I'm a local. Of course, I know the best brew pub in town. But why on earth would they take a chance on me?"

I go with the truth. "First, I'll vouch for you and so will my boss, Tara. She's seen the footage I've sent and is dying to see you perform in person. Second, she is quite interested in finding local talent. I also know they're desperate for someone to fill in because my sister was talking about it just last night. The woman they had lined up had a family emergency and had to leave town for a few weeks."

The confident man I watched perform last night is still there, I can sense it. But his expression is pensive and frankly, I'd almost say he looks scared, as he stares at me wordlessly.

It's time to go big, or go home, so I lay it all on the line. "Jax, the Monday night crowd won't even be as big as last night. What do you say? Do you think you have another performance in you?"

My thundering heart makes the seconds tick by slowly. I have no idea what he'll say in response. But I won't let myself say another word, until he's had the chance to think it over.

After what seems like forever, Jax counters with a knowing smirk. "I'll do this gig tomorrow night... under one condition."

I'm sure I can make whatever he needs happen, so I raise my chin and refuse to back down. "And what's that?"

"You let me take you out afterward."

Holy shit. I was not expecting that.

Chapter 4
Jax

As I sit on stage, singing my heart out, I'm energized like I've never been before. I've always loved music, but the way Sloane's looking at me pushes me to take things up a notch. I'm playing a mixture of cover songs I know are crowd favorites, while sliding in some of my own to test things out.

Each time I dart my eyes to Sloane, I grow more confident that I'm not making a complete ass of myself on stage. I wasn't sure what I was getting myself into, but now that I'm here, I'll admit this is something I could get used to.

There's an energy I can't describe flowing through me. I've never experimented with drugs, but I'm sure it's like someone who's taken a hit of heroin, and I'm riding a high of pure adrenaline. With each new song I sing, the crowd gets more into it, which only drives my energy further.

When I launch into a cover of "Girls Like You" by Maroon 5, Sloane's eyes lock onto mine. The musical intro is catchy, and thankfully, I know this song like the back of my hand. Giving her a wink, I purposely change up the first words to let her know I'm interested in getting to know her better. "It's been twenty-four hours... I need more hours... with you."

Her brows fly to her hairline, then a slow smile spreads across her face as she waits to see what I'll say next.

Yeah, she knows I'm talking about her.

I may not know her well, but I do know she keeps me on my toes. I'm dying to see if I can get her to let her hair down and relax a bit. Don't get me wrong, Sloane's hot as fuck in those pencil skirts and fancy shirts with her hair and makeup making her look like she's stepped off a runway, but I'm more interested in getting to know the side of her she doesn't let others see too often. It slipped out while we were having breakfast—especially when she talks about her family. My gut tells me there's so much more to her than she's let me see. It may take some time, but she'll soon find I'm patient enough to wait her out.

When I launch into the chorus, she's still got that camera up and rolling, so I ignore it and continue singing this song to her, keeping the remaining lyrics as they were intended. I don't know Sloane in the way this song describes, but if she'll give me the chance, I'd like to.

As if I can't help myself, when this song ends, I launch into Dave Matthews' "Crash Into Me." The crowd immediately recognizes it and cheers enthusiastically. This wasn't what was on my set list, but I found myself strumming the chords before I could stop myself.

Sloane's eyes never leave mine as I leave everything on the stage in this performance.

Holy shit—this song is so sexual.

I've never played it looking into someone's eyes like this. My nerves are on fire as I make it to the bridge.

Sloane's on her feet, swaying to the music, and I swear it might as well be only the two of us out here—she's all I see. Fuck, she even brushes her fingers along her lips when I sing about giving me a hint of how she's feeling. The moment I get to the point in the song where I'm apologizing for being so lost in her, I don't even feel guilty—though I probably should. She's fucking beautiful and completely mesmerizing. What I'd give to hold her close and get completely lost in her.

Holy fucking shit, when I sing about hiking up her skirt, that little brat arches a brow as she slyly plays with the hem of her own.

Oh, Jesus. Help me. I am so fucking screwed with this girl.

I nearly lose track of the next lines, but I recover before anyone notices.

I sure as fuck didn't peg her for flirting back. But I'm here for it.

I wonder what else she's hiding behind that "All business exterior" she holds on to so well.

Oh, Sloane. If you keep that up, I just might have to show you what it's like to crash into me. I barely know her, but if I'm feeling the sexual tension between us in a crowded room, I'm not sure I'll survive when I finally get her alone.

Needing to change things up and relieve myself from the sexual tension building between Sloane and myself and finish this set without showing the world what she does to me, I launch into singing "Sweet Home Alabama." Then I throw in a few of the ones I've written to balance things out. It feels great to try out the songs I've kept hidden for so long, making me wonder—*why have I waited so long to do this?*

Time flies and before I know it, my time on stage is over. Thankfully, by the time I sing my last note, my nerves are long gone. I'm certain I owe it all to Sloane.

I'm surprised when the owner of the bar meets me as I get off stage. I'd spoken to him briefly before and didn't expect for him to stick around. He'd mentioned something about getting home early tonight.

As I step closer, he takes my hand firmly in his and gives it a good shake. "That was fantastic. You were brilliant tonight. I'd love for you to do this again."

"Thanks for having me. It's a great crowd."

Nodding, he grins. "Yeah…" he draws out as he looks around. "But they were sure into you. Sloane mentioned you work at Stella's. Any chance we can work a deal, and you'd become my regular entertainment for Monday and Thursday nights?"

Holy shit. Is he for real? What do I even say?

Before I can answer, he throws in, "It'll be three hundred per week, through the end of summer."

Dumbfounded, I blurt out, "For sets like this?" Hell, I only played a little over two hours. With an offer like that, how can I refuse? I'm certain I can work this out with my manager. After all, he could switch me to days on the nights I play here. I won't leave him stranded.

Nodding once, he says, "Yeah. Would that work for you?"

"I head back to school in September. I'll have to talk with my manager at Stella's, but I think I can make this work."

With a big grin, he pats me on the shoulder. "You tell Nathan… he owes me. I helped him find that manager of his. He can share some of his talent."

That's living in a small town for you.

With a chuckle, I say, "Okay, Mr. Redlin. I'll let them both know."

Swatting his hand in the air, Mr. Redlin guffaws, "None of that, Mr. Redlin nonsense. Call me Joe. Mr. Redlin's my dad, and he's still alive and kicking at nearly ninety."

"Well, that's good to know." I laugh. "I'll be sure to let Nathan know about returning the favor. In the meantime, I already have Thursday off, so count me in for then."

Someone calls Joe's name from behind us, and Joe gestures

for them to wait a minute. "Look, I gotta take care of something. But I'll see you Thursday. Come a little early, so we can fill out some paperwork."

"Sounds like a plan, Joe. See you then."

With a bounce in my step, I make my way over to Sloane.

She's looking down at her phone, but the moment she sees me, she eagerly stands from the table to close the distance between us. "You were spectacular tonight. I can't wait to edit some of these clips to share them with you. You really killed it. I think they ate up your originals just as well as the cover songs."

"Thanks. I think so, too." Tilting my head to the parking lot as I hitch the strap of my guitar case higher on my shoulder, I ask, "You ready to get out of here?"

Reaching for her purse, she grins. "Got any place in mind?"

Letting out a long breath, I admit, "I'm too keyed up to sit anywhere. Mind if we take a walk?"

She darts her tongue out and slides it along her lower lip as a smile plays at the corner of her lips. "I think I can handle that."

Chapter 5
Sloane

Either Jax isn't being straight with me, or the man's got more talent in his pinky than most do in a lifetime. He was on fire tonight. I wasn't kidding when I told him I got some great footage. I can't wait to show both him and my boss the final edits.

He's an absolute dream to record as the camera ate him up. His voice is smooth as butter, with a touch of gravel, which I'm sure made ovaries throughout the crowd burst. His raw talent and charisma on stage makes him the whole package. It doesn't hurt that he's easy on the eyes either. Once he fine tunes his brand, I'm certain everyone will line up to watch him perform. If I have any say, in the very near future—Jax Cartwright will be huge!

As we walk to his truck to drop off his guitar, his pent-up energy rolls off him in waves and creeps into the crevices of my soul. I can't quite describe what I'm feeling, but suddenly, I'm fully aware of everything Jax. From the light bounce in his step, to the sway of his arm as he walks. I'm completely in tune with his every movement, and my body zings with anticipation of what's to come.

With his truck parked along the street, he quickly deposits his guitar inside the lockbox in the bed of his truck and turns to face me with an eager smile. Glancing at my messenger bag, he asks, "Wanna put that in your car so we can wander and relax a bit?"

"I walked here tonight, so I'm good." Clutching it as if it's my lifeline, I blow out a loud breath. "Everything I might need is in this bag. You never know when inspiration will hit. Besides, Tara might need something from me, and I should keep it handy."

Shaking his head, a smile pulls at his lips. "Oh, Sloane, you can't work *all* the time..." I watch as his face turns pensive for the briefest of moments, and I'm certain he's plotting. Suddenly, one brow quirks in my direction, as a smirk rolls across his face.

I know without a doubt, I'm in so much trouble with this man.

Running a hand along his jaw, he casually asks, "What will it take to get you to turn off that brilliant brain of yours and just walk with me?"

My traitorous body reacts without my permission as a swarm of warmth flutters deep in my belly. I'm unsure what to make of it and have no idea how to react. He's barely known me a few days and already gets me at my core—my brain doesn't turn off.

Maybe it's just an assumption. But the look in his eyes clearly shows he wants to take the time to know the real me.

Why is this both equally flattering and terrifying?

Reaching his hand out, he gestures for my bag. "Well, if we're going to schlep that thing around while we walk, would you at least let me carry it?"

"That's completely unnecessary," I insist, hoisting it higher across my body. "I'm perfectly capable of carrying my own bag."

Sighing heavily, he shakes his head. "I *know* you're capable...Never meant to insinuate otherwise. But for the record, it doesn't mean you have to. I merely offered because I thought it would give you the opportunity to let your hair down and relax, which at this point, I'm sure is a rarity."

"I can relax," flies out of my mouth so fast, even I don't believe it.

Clearly, neither does he.

Crossing his arms over his chest, he challenges, "Okay... prove it. Tell me one thing you've done for yourself in the last week that had nothing to do with work... where you one hundred percent unplugged and allowed yourself to relax."

Rolling my lip between my teeth, I look to the sky as I run through the events of this past week. Finally, when one pops into my head, I grin. "I watched my sister Raven surf the other morning."

Eying me suspiciously, he asks, "You expect me to believe you actually sat on the beach and did nothing but watch her surf?"

Shit. He's got me there. "Well... I did answer some emails while she caught some waves. It's harder than you think to just sit and watch someone for nearly an hour."

"I'll have to take your word for it. But that still means you worked." Pointing in the direction of the beach, he asks, "Wanna walk along the Prom?"

Knowing the Promenade is one of the longer walking paths in Seaside that's well-lit and filled with people at all hours, I nod in agreement. It's not quite dark, but the sun will set soon. "Sounds good."

Once we're walking, I switch the subject to him. "So, tell me, Jax... what's something you consider fun to do in Seaside?"

"Well, since I've been home for the summer, I haven't had a lot of free time. But I do like to hike and do the ropes course. I also go to bonfires at the beach and anything that keeps me away from the downtown crowds in the summer. I've mainly spent time alone just playing music—as I'm sure you could've guessed."

Bumping my hip into him as we walk along the sidewalk, I tease, "Yeah, I thought music might be in there. You sure you're not holding back on me about performing in public? The way you played tonight was better than most I've seen."

"Thanks," he sighs heavily. "I'm not sure what got into me tonight—but I'm nowhere used to playing in public. I still can't believe Joe wants to make this a regular thing. But I'm not a fool, and I won't turn down the money offered. I can use every cent for college this fall."

Just as we make it to the Prom, a bicyclist zooms past, and Jax quickly places a hand on my lower back, guiding me around them, as well as the next girl enjoying her evening ride. The moment we're in the clear, his hand drops, and I'm left feeling a sense of loss.

Why do I miss his touch? That makes no sense.

Shaking my head to clear my ridiculous thoughts, I ask the first question that pops into my mind, "So... you're planning to be a computer engineer and a closet musician? How exactly will that work?"

The low chuckle Jax releases makes me smile in return. "Well, I wouldn't put it like that. But yeah, I'm graduating next year with my bachelor's in computer engineering. I've always been interested in technology and well... music is just something I've done since living in the dorms. My roommate taught me the basics on the guitar, and while he was away one week-end, it just sort of is something I picked up."

Is he kidding me?

"Uh, something you just picked up...eh? Well, lucky for us you did because you're an insanely talented musician."

"I wouldn't go that far, Sloane. But thanks."

Does he really not see it?

It's endearing how modest he is. But instead of praising him further, I ask another question I've been dying to know since the day we met. "How does your dad fit into all of this? You mentioned something about your performance being a promise to your dad... what did you mean by that?"

Shrugging, he grins. "You noticed that tidbit, did you?"

Uh, I've noticed everything about you.

Thankfully, my brain catches up to my mouth, and I manage a challenge. "Are you gonna tell me, or is this some family secret you're taking to the grave?"

This earns me a deep belly laugh.

God, this man is gorgeous when he smiles.

"No, Sloane, it's not a family secret." Taking a deep breath, he slowly exhales. "And I'm certainly not taking it to the grave... dramatic much? Seriously though, it's more of a chal-lenge he's pushed upon me."

"What do you mean, challenge?" I ask, my curiosity piqued.

"To make a *really* long story short, my dad is one of the best men I know. From the moment he found out Mom was preg-nant with me, he's always taken the safe route. His entire goal was to provide for our family, no matter the sacrifices he had to make personally..." He trails off as he walks toward the cement railing along the Prom and stares out at the ocean.

"He sounds like a wonderful man," I prompt, hoping he'll share more.

"Yeah, he really is," he says on a sigh, as he watches a seagull land a few feet below us in the sand. "One time when I was younger, I used to love visiting him at work at the mill. Like most boys my age, I loved heavy equipment and wanted to drive them when I got older. I couldn't think of a better job in the world. Then one day, I asked him if he liked working at the mill. I'll never forget the look on his face—as it was evident, he didn't. But he never complained; he simply explained it the best way he could. He said, '*You know, Jax, sometimes it isn't about loving the job. It's more about providing for those you love.*'"

Jax is quiet for a moment, and I watch patiently as he rolls his lower lip between his teeth. Eventually, he shakes his head and meets my gaze. "The answer to your question will make more sense now that you know that bit of backstory." Letting out a long breath, he slowly smiles. "You see... Dad came home from work one day early this summer and heard me playing on our back deck. I have no idea how long he listened to me play, as I thought I was alone. I'd been working on one of my songs and so entranced in the process, I didn't even see him. When I finally got the song exactly how I wanted it and played it through for myself, I was met with a slow and steady clap—which nearly scared the piss out of me." Jax chuckles, and I can't help but join him as I picture the scene.

"Dad walked onto the deck with an expression I couldn't quite read. He'd been smiling one minute and the next, he was more serious than I'd ever seen him. He asked how long I'd been playing, and I told him I'd picked it up a few years ago. Then he asked why he'd never heard me play before."

Invested in his story, I blurt out, "What'd you tell him?"

Shrugging, he grins impishly as he runs a hand through his hair. "The truth. It was just something I did for fun. Then he said something completely out of character. He told me he'd never seen me look so happy and that if I'm interested in playing music, I should take my shot. I'm young and can always fall back on my original plans. Other than getting my degree, I have no responsibilities, or anyone relying on me, and why not do something I'm passionate about."

Wondering if I'd missed him in the crowd, I ask, "Was he there on open mic night?"

"No. He and Mom are celebrating their anniversary this week on an Alaskan cruise. It's something she's always wanted to do, so he surprised her."

"That's amazing. But how is this out of character for him? He seems so thoughtful."

"Dad's always been supportive. It's how I became the first one in my family to attend college. But he isn't the *take your shot and follow your dreams* type of guy. He's always been you want something—work your ass off for it."

"That's my dad's motto. It's probably why I graduated a year early," I quickly add.

"They'd probably get along then," he surmises. "But to answer your question, Dad had a mild heart attack last year. He's always been a planner, a saver, and worked his ass off. He's expected me and my sister to do the same. I guess he's realized you can't take it with you when you're gone... and now he basically lives by the motto of *you've only got one life to live—so make it count.*"

"I'm sure a heart attack will do that to you."

"Yeah, it sure does. Thankfully, he's fully recovered and expects to have a long life ahead of him. According to Dad, he plans to make the most of it. Mom couldn't be happier. She gets to travel and see the things she's always wanted to see. He's still got a few years before he can retire, but they make their vacations count."

"Have you told your parents about performing?"

Shaking his head, he shrugs. "No, I needed to do this on my own. Once they're back in town, I'm sure they'll come watch—especially since I'll have a regular gig at Pop's..." Suddenly, he lets out a low sound, something between a laugh and a grunt and shakes his head. "Huh... a regular gig... Never thought I'd hear those words coming out of my mouth."

"Well, you should. I think this will be the start of something amazing for you, Jax."

"Hmmmm... I'm not one to jinx anything. So, let's just see how this goes."

When a group of high schoolers come and gather at a bench nearby, I point in the direction of the path. "Wanna keep walking?"

He doesn't say a word, but once again, his hand rests on my lower back as we maneuver our way around the crowd. My spine tingles, and again, I'm hypersensitive to everything Jax. As if the universe is against me, the wind picks up at this exact moment, making my mouth water as his heavenly scent washes over me.

What the hell is this man wearing? I swear, whatever it is, it's laced with the most toxic pheromones I've ever experienced. I've been around him before, and he always smells good, but tonight—well, this is next level. Leaning in a little closer, I allow myself to slowly inhale, capturing it to memory.

Once we're clear of the crowd, he drops his hand again and steps to the left, putting some distance between us. I'm not sure if it's a guy thing, or a Jax thing, but his protective instincts spark something inside me that I'd long forgotten and makes me realize I may be perfectly fine on my own, but I do miss intimacy.

"So..." he draws out, breaking my trance. "Tell me, Sloane, when you're not working, what do you actually do for fun?"

Shrugging, I admit on a heavy sigh, "I don't really have

much of a life beyond work. During the summers, I spend as much time as I can with my sisters. We usually just cook meals together, watch movies, hang at the beach, or lounge around the house when we get a free night. Since Lanie first went away to college, we've made it a priority to spend our summers together. Then when Raven and I took off to Gonzaga, it became even more important—especially for Lizzy. If we don't make family a priority, we'd never see one another."

"Is Lizzy the youngest?"

"Yep. She's the baby—though she just completed her first year at Portland State. I guess she's not a baby anymore."

Chuckling, he agrees, "No, she isn't. But my younger sister Emily will always be the baby of our family, no matter how old she gets. She'll be a senior in high school next year. I can't imagine what it was like to live with three siblings growing up. I love Em, but we're far enough apart that we tend to not have a lot in common."

"I can't imagine life without my sisters," I gush. "Maybe it's because we were forced to be each other's best friends, or it happened naturally. But they're my ride or die, and there's not much I wouldn't do for them."

Turning to face me, he asks, "Do you have a sister you're closest with?"

"Yep. Raven—hands down. She's my culprit in crime and my other half. We couldn't be more opposite on many things, but she's my person."

"I thought you weren't supposed to have favorites?" he teases.

"Yeah..." I draw out, searching for words that could explain our connection. "Don't get me wrong, I love my other sisters and would kill for them if necessary, but Raven and I are so closely wound, my mom used to tease that I'd get the box of tissues ready before she'd sneeze."

"That's..." he draws out as if he's unsure what to say. Then after a few heartbeats, he blinks his eyes and admits, "A little freaky."

Laughing at his bemused expression, I agree, "You're right. It is. But It's just so much of who I am, I don't even think twice about it."

"Are all of you connected like that?"

"Nope. Just Raven and me. I think we would've done our parents in if we all had telepathic senses. We already outnumbered them, especially after their divorce. Dad had to use his military training to keep us in line... and Mom... well... now that we're all older, we recognize her for the saint she is. Though truth be told, they both made raising four kids look easy—even though I'm sure it was anything but."

"I can't imagine." Jax shakes his head.

When I look up, I realize we've been walking so long, we're almost to my house. Seeing all the lights are on and my sisters are hanging out in the kitchen, I give Jax fair warning. "That's me, right there."

Cocking his head to the side, he asks, "This is the house you visited each summer?"

"For as long as I can remember. Why?"

I can hear the wonder in his voice as he admits, "Wow. I can't tell you how many times I've walked right by this place. It's a wonder our paths haven't crossed earlier."

"Do you live near here?" I ask, wondering just how often he passed by. I would've noticed Jax. I'm certain of that.

"No, I live at the other end of town. But my buddies and I used the Prom as a shortcut to get to one another's houses before we started driving."

"Sloane? Is that you?" I hear a male voice call from behind, causing me to jump back from Jax. I hadn't realized my body had crept closer to him.

Turning, I smile at Ryan approaching. He's sweaty and must've been out for a run. But I quickly make introductions before he jumps to any conclusions. "Hey, Ry, how's it going? You remember Jax, right?"

Reaching out his hand, Jax offers it to Ryan. "Great to see you, man. It's been awhile."

"You were great at open mic. I had no idea you could sing like that. You still at Berkeley?" Ryan asks with interest.

"Thanks. It was a first. I'm just home for the summer."

Looking from me to Jax, Ryan asks, "What are you two up to?"

"Jax just got himself a regular gig at Pop's. Lanie will get to experience his talents all summer long," I proudly inform Ryan.

"Wow. Congratulations. I'm sure the crowd will love you. Lanie and Sloane couldn't stop talking about your performance the other night."

He cocks a brow in my direction. "Is that right?"

Fuck... I don't want him to get the wrong impression. "We were just talking about how insanely talented you were, and how I got you to perform again tonight. It's not that big of a deal."

Ryan glances at the house and notices Lanie plop down on the couch in the living room. "Look, I'll catch you later. Lanie and I have a movie night planned, and I need a shower. It was great seeing you, man. I'm sure I'll see you around."

Like a moth to a flame, Ryan doesn't even wait for a response before bee-lining it up the path into the house. That man is so in love with my sister, it's like she's the only one he sees.

Rocking back on his heels, Jax watches Ryan hop up the steps to the deck and bound into the house. "Well, I should let you hang out with your family. Thanks again for encouraging me to perform tonight. It was a lot of fun."

"I wouldn't have missed it for the world. I can't wait to see you again Thursday night."

Jax stares at me for the longest moment. His body leans closer to mine. The tension that's been shifting between us all night is back with a vengeance. I know without a doubt he's about to lean in and kiss me; I'll have no choice but to kiss him back.

Suddenly, a shout comes from my house, "Want us to save the movie for you?"

Could my family have worse timing?

It feels like a needle scratching across vinyl as I watch him blink and pull away. "I'd better let you get in there. But, Sloane... for the record..." He leans in closer, and I can barely remember how to breathe. But instead of kissing me, he smirks. "I'll be asking you what you did to unplug the next time I see you. You'd better be able to tell me you've done something just for you."

"Uh... Bossy much?" I sputter, trying to come up with a comeback and utterly fail. Now I sound like I'm twelve.

Laughing, Jax turns and starts walking away, but after a few steps, he stops and glances over his shoulder with a challenge, "Oh, Sloane. You have no idea just how bossy I can be. I guess you'll just have to hang out with me more to find out."

Without letting me say another word, he pivots and walks away, and the only thing I can think of is *yeah, I'd like to see you try.*

Chapter 6
Sloane

I'll give my sister Lanie some credit for her restraint. We make it nearly twenty-five minutes into the movie before she turns to me with a pointed stare. At first, she just silently scrutinizes me. I feel her gaze, but I do my best to ignore her and watch the movie. Then she finally breaks and blurts out, "So, what's up with you and Jax?"

With popcorn halfway to my mouth, I stop and stare, wondering where she's going with this. "What do you mean?"

Giving me a look only an older sister can perfect from watching my mom, she chastises me, "You know exactly what I mean. What's going on with the two of you?"

"I'm helping him gain exposure. I think he's just the type we're looking for in terms of local talent for the festival later this summer."

Arching a brow, she tries another approach. "You've never let anyone else you work with walk you home. What gives?"

Yeah, that's a good question, but I quickly protest before she can make more of it. "It's not what you think. He was amped up after killing it on stage. We went for a walk. When we ended up near the house, I came inside. End of story."

Lizzy points out, "You've never let anyone else you've just met come close to knowing where we live. I'm thinking there's somethin' special about this one, don't ya think, Lanie?"

"Oh, I think so, too," Lanie taunts, then asks another question I don't have the answer to, "Why did you feel the need to walk with him in the first place? Don't musicians usually blow off steam after performances in the bedroom?"

Ryan grumbles, "Did you have to go there, Lanie? The dude is someone I went to school with."

Shrugging, Lanie giggles. "Sorry."

But I ignore them both as I sigh heavily. "You have no idea what you're talking about." Looking between my sisters, I shake my head. "Clearly, you're delusional. There's no point in arguing about this, so let's get back to the movie." Doing my best to move on, I pop another piece of popcorn into my mouth.

"Well, you didn't see the look on your face when you came inside tonight," Lanie points out. "I'm certain there's more to Jax than you're letting on."

To Lanie, Lizzy asks, "What does Jax look like anyway? I wish I had gone with you to open mic. From the sounds of it, I missed out on something good. Will he be performing again?"

Knowing Lanie will find out soon enough, I fill her in on tonight's events. "Joe asked him to fill in on Monday and Thursday nights at Pop's Hops."

"Really?" Lanie's eyes light up. "I know he's been trying to fill the spot since Tracy is out of town dealing with her family. Does this mean I'll get to see you those nights if I'm working, too?"

"Probably," I admit, not wanting to make a big deal of things. "I need to get some footage to share on social media if I want to build up his hype before the contest."

"You still didn't answer my question," Lizzy insists. "What does this guy look like? Sloane looked so lost in thought when she came inside. I feel like I'm missing something."

"Don't you have a video of Jax?" Ryan suggests. "You know as well as I do, we'll never watch this movie if you don't give in to your sisters' demands."

Where is Raven when I need her? It's like they're all ganging up on me. Clearly, I'm outnumbered. But Ryan's got a point. Quickly, I dig into my pocket and fish out my phone. After scrolling for one of his better shots, I turn my phone in the direction of Lizzy, hoping she'll back off.

"Hot damn," she draws out, pretending to fan herself. "If you're not interested, do you think you can introduce me?"

Oh, hell no. I've gotta shut this down. "Uh, don't you think you're a little young for him?"

Lifting her chin, Lizzy holds my gaze and pointedly reminds me, "I'm just a little over a year younger than you. Does that mean *you're* too young for him?"

"Liz, he's a senior in college, and I just graduated. I'm a better fit for him in that department. Besides, I'll be twenty-one this fall."

Lanie waggles her brows as a wide grin spreads across her face. "Oh, so you are a good fit for him?"

Shit. I walked right into that one.

"Not the point," I mutter as the room fills with laughter.

Normally, I'd welcome the teasing—but not when it's directed toward me.

Waving a hand in the air, Lizzy assures me, "Oh, don't worry, Sloane. You may not want to admit it, but I'm certain he's your type. Heck, maybe he'll be just what you need to get that stick out of your ass and have fun. I've heard musicians have a wild side to them."

"You know I don't date musicians. They're too flighty.

Besides, it's not smart to crap where I eat. I've got too much riding on this internship to let anything get in the way. Though, fun fact... Jax is a computer engineer, who until recently, has only been a closet musician. Though if I have anything to say about it, he won't stay hidden for long."

"Seriously? A guy as hot as that, is a computer geek?" Lizzy practically shouts. "Maybe I need to hang out in the computer science department. Who knew?"

Ryan pipes in, "You'd be surprised who you'll find in the various engineering departments."

Lanie pats his face and teases her adorable boyfriend. "Oh, sweetie, it's adorable when you're jealous. But don't worry, I've only got the hots for you."

Rolling his eyes, he swats her hand away. "I'm not fishing for compliments, Lanie. Just pointing out facts."

"Good, because even though I've only got eyes for you, it doesn't mean Jax isn't a good-looking guy. I'd have to be blind or dead not to notice."

"So noted." Ryan nods once with a solemn face, making us laugh.

"Well, now that it's clear what you all think of Jax, wanna get back to the movie?"

"You're just lucky Raven's not here, or she'd know exactly what you're *not* saying about Jax." Lanie taunts before adding, "But mark my words, I'm certain there's something more going on with Sloane... but don't worry, we'll let you keep your secrets —for now."

THE NEXT MORNING, when I come down for my much-needed dose of caffeine, I'm surprised to already find coffee brewed and Ryan sitting at the island, staring into his mug as if it has all the answers he's looking for.

Not wanting to startle him, I offer a greeting as I approach. "Mornin'."

"Hey, Sloane, you're up early."

"Couldn't sleep, so I thought I'd get a jump on my day." I shrug as I shuffle through the kitchen, heading straight for the cupboard with the mugs. The sun has barely made its appearance and usually, he has the kitchen to himself at this hour. He looked so lost in thought. I wonder what's got him so pensive.

"Everything okay?" I ask once I've filled my cup and grab creamer from the fridge.

"Yeah... just thinking." He lets out a slow breath.

"About?" I probe, knowing I won't push things too far but wanting to lend an ear if he needs one.

Suddenly, he goes from sullen to perky. "Hey, you might just be the one to help."

"I can try my best," I offer, taking the stool beside him.

"Look, out of all the sisters, I know you'll keep my secret if it means surprising Lanie."

He's got a point. Lizzy can't keep secrets for shit, and Raven will spill the beans if she thinks it's necessary. But there's no sense in discussing it, so I cut to the chase, "Go on..."

"I've already talked with your dad, and I've had a ring that's burning a hole in my pocket for the last month or so."

Holy shit. This is huge. I knew things between my sister and Ryan were heading this way, but I didn't know when it would happen. "Seriously, you talked to Dad? How did that go?"

Chuckling, Ryan shakes his head. "Better than expected. I've had a ring in my pocket since graduation, but nothing's felt right, in terms of timing," He frowns, making my heart sink for him. "I'd love to do something at Pop's this next week as it's the anniversary of our first date."

Ryan is so perfect for Lanie.

"What did you have in mind?" I ask, hoping to get enough information to elicit decent advice for this situation.

"I don't have a freaking clue. I'm thinking about taking her to dinner and maybe catching a performance while we're at it. She'll never expect it. Do you think I could talk Jax into playing Ed Sheeran's, 'Thinking Out Loud?' It's one of her favorites, and she'd never expect a proposal at the end."

"We'll never know unless we ask," I point out, as my entire body wants to squeal with excitement for my sister, but I manage to stifle my emotions as I'd likely wake my sisters.

Lanie's going to lose her shit. I know Ryan is it for her, but I don't think she's expecting him to take things to the next level so soon. She's been adamant about finishing school and starting her career.

Ryan's quiet, and I watch as he works out whatever is rolling around in his brain. Finally, he breaks the silence by clearing his throat. "The thing is, I know Jax but not that well. Do you think you could help me set something up?"

"Is that all you need from me?" Surely, there's more.

Nodding, he grins impishly. "I've been rehearsing what I'll say for weeks. But I could use his help to make it special. I know Lanie's not big on being the center of attention, but I have to do this at Pop's. After all—it's where I scored my first date with her."

Hearing someone move around from upstairs, I whisper, "You let me take care of Jax. He's there twice a week for the summer, so just let me know when you need this to happen, and we'll make it work."

Hearing someone on the stairs, I quickly blurt out so only Ryan can hear, "Do you mind if I invite my sisters?"

Placing a hand on mine, he gives it a squeeze. "I wouldn't have it any other way."

Chapter 7
Jax

I'm flying high as I work through the last of my set. Sloane's been recording every song and even though I have yet to see any footage, I know deep in my heart, I'm on fire again tonight. Right before I went on, she asked if we could talk when I finish. Time was running short, so I didn't get the details as to what she wants to talk about, and it's driving me crazy wondering what it could be.

Tonight, I've mixed more of my own songs into the set. I started out nervous, especially when I'd throw in something the crowd had never heard. Thankfully, by the end, I find my groove and slay it. It feels freaking incredible. They're practically eating out of my hands and don't want me to stop.

The moment I hop off stage, Sloane's there to greet me with excitement written all over that gorgeous face of hers. Opening her arms, I walk right into them as if I've been doing it for years, swooping her into a hug and spinning her around as she gushes, "You were amazing tonight, Jax. I swear you just keep getting better."

Squeezing her tight, energy zings through me. I want this

moment to last forever. Musical high, beautiful girl, and ohmigod—this woman smells amazing. I truly can't get enough.

Reluctantly, my brain catches up with my body. Before things get awkward, I set her back on the floor. Once I'm sure she's steady, I let go, and words gush out of my mouth. "Thanks. It felt like I was on fire tonight. Songs kept flowing, and the crowd just ate them up. I can't believe how fast the set was. I swear I blinked, and it was over."

Her beautiful laugh rings out above the noise of the crowd. "I can imagine." Briefly, she looks toward her sister waiting on a couple a few tables down. Then she leans in close, almost conspiratorially, in a low voice so only I can hear, and asks, "Can I talk to you alone for a minute?" When she glances again in her sister's direction, I can tell something's up.

Without hesitation, I reach for her hand, pulling her away from the crowd and toward my truck where I can deposit my guitar and give her my full attention.

Once we're out of earshot from everyone, I ask, "What's up?"

For the briefest of moments, she glances back at the crowd, then her eyes cut to mine. "Look. I might as well be straight with you. I need a favor."

What could she possibly want from me?

Then it dawns on me that she keeps looking back. "You keep looking over there like something's wrong. Need me to take care of someone for you?"

"No. I just need a favor, and I don't want my sister to hear."

"What kind of favor?" I draw out, as I watch her glance back at the crowd once more. Sloane's normally quite serious and to the point. What has her acting this way?

"Well, the favor's not really for me. It's for Ryan."

"Why isn't Ryan asking this for himself?" I wonder. He and I weren't super close, but it's a small town, and we all get along.

"I told him I'd take care of this for him, so it could stay a surprise. You see, he wants to propose to Lanie." Again, she glances over her shoulder at her sister.

"Good for him. What does this have to do with me?"

"I told you he and Lanie met last summer. Well, it was one year ago next week that he walked into that very bar while she was working. After he ate, he convinced her to go on their first date. He'd love to propose at Pop's as it's a special place for them."

Utterly confused, I ask, "Where do I fit in? Why does he need a favor from me, specifically?"

"It's simple. He wants to propose during one of the songs they first heard you play at open mic."

Well, this is flattering. "Which one?"

"Lanie's favorite artist is Ed Sheeran. Could you play 'Thinking Out Loud' at your set next week, so he can propose during it?"

Chuckling, I shake my head. "You sure have a big buildup for a simple request. Of course, I'll play the song. Just let me know when he's ready. Anything else?"

"No, Ryan's got everything covered. Though I do need to figure out how to get my sisters here without clueing Lanie in."

I can see the wheels spinning in that beautiful brain of hers. I wonder if she ever takes a break. This prompts me to quickly change the subject. "Speaking of planning, what have you done for yourself since I walked you home?"

"Uh, does sleep count?"

"Not really the point." I chuckle. Damn, this girl needs help if that's all she does for herself. "What are your plans tomorrow afternoon?"

The way she rolls her eyes to the sky, I'm sure she's mentally going through her never-ending to-do list. "I'm not sure. Why?"

"Can you spare a few hours from that crazy schedule of yours?"

It's adorable how her lips purse, and she squints, scrutinizing my every movement. Like I'd give my thoughts away so easily.

Nope. I can play this game all day, Sloane.

"Are you busy or not?" I challenge.

"I don't know," she draws out, her eyes narrowing further. "It depends."

Oh, this girl needs to learn to let loose.

"You're either busy or not. It's simple."

Placing her hand on her hip, she volleys back, just as I'd expect. "What time, specifically? Afternoon is rather vague..." she trails off, and I find myself stepping closer.

"Six o'clock." Surely, she's done with work by then.

"Does this involve eating?"

Oh-my-freaking-God.

This woman is infuriating. *Can't she just say yes or no?*

My nerves are already wound tight from tonight's show and bantering with her has me on the verge of losing what little control I have left. She has no idea just how much I want to lean in and kiss that smirk right off her face.

The tension between us grows higher as I raise a brow and counter, "It can."

For the longest time, she just stares at me. Just when I think she's going to turn me down, her head slowly nods once, as one word escapes from her lips. "Fine."

Relief floods through me faster than a crack in the Hoover Dam.

Not wanting to give anything away, I keep my expression locked in place.

"I'll pick you up at six..." Looking her over from head to toe, I slowly take in what I now consider her work uniform—

another button-up shirt and pencil skirt. Damn, she's gorgeous. But this won't do for what I have in mind. I quickly add, "Dress casual. You can do that, right?"

Letting out a huff, she says, "Again, you need to be more specific. Casual can range from a summer dress to beach attire in this town."

"As hot as you'd look in a dress..." My eyes roam to her sexy long legs, imagining what they'd look like under a flowy summer dress, I want her to be comfortable. I quickly remind her, "It's cold at night, so beach casual will do."

Cocking her head to the side, she raises one of her perfectly sculped brows back at me. "And you're not going to tell me what our plans are?"

Crossing my arms over my chest to keep from reaching for her, I shake my head. "Nope. I've got a feeling you need a little spontaneity in your life, so it's best I keep you on your toes."

Chapter 8
Sloane

As I throw another outfit onto my bed, I groan in frustration and stomp back to my closet. "Why the hell couldn't he tell me what our plans are? It's not like I'm asking him for our national secrets. How the hell can I be prepared if he doesn't clue me in?"

"Is that a rhetorical question?" Raven asks, scaring the shit out of me. I thought I had the house to myself, but she must've gotten off work early.

Clutching my hand to my chest to catch my breath, I blurt out, "What are you doing here?"

"Uh... I live here. What's going on? I haven't seen you so worked up about anything in forever."

"I'm not worked up," I protest as I go back to looking over my selection of clothes from my closet.

"Sure... you're not," Raven deadpans. "Your room always looks as if it's been hit by a tornado."

Walking to meet me by the closet, she asks, "Who's got your panties in such a twist that you have nearly every article of clothing you own strewn across your bed?"

"My panties aren't in a twist," I chastise. I always know what to wear. I have no idea why I'm having such a hard time today. "If you were told to wear something beach casual, what would you wear?"

Raven has the audacity to say something sensible. "Uh... jeans and a graphic tee, with a hoodie for when it gets cold."

"Nothing looks right though," I moan, pointing to the pile of clothes strewn across my bed.

I start turning toward my dresser, but Raven stops me. "Sloaney, what gives? Clearly, there's more to this than picking out an outfit. This is me you're talking to. I felt the tension rolling off you the moment I stepped into the house. I came to find out what's wrong."

"Stupid Jax challenged me to dress in something casual. I at least got him to clarify beach casual, but now I'm left wondering exactly what the hell that means."

Don't think I don't notice the way her lips tip at the edges, and she's fighting a smile. But thankfully, she thinks better of it and schools her features. I'm in no mood to be made fun of.

"Who is this *stupid Jax* you speak of?"

"I don't have time for this," I mutter. "He'll be here in less than an hour."

"I've got twenty minutes before I'm meeting up with Dan, a guy I met earlier today at work. We're meeting at the Thai restaurant downtown. I'll give ten minutes to solving this crisis of yours. I'm the queen of casual, as you well know. I'm sure I can help."

"*Casual hookups* are more like it," I mutter. She knows I'm not throwing shade. I love her to pieces. In fact, I wish I could be more like Raven sometimes.

She's someone who goes with the flow and doesn't over-analyze things to death. I swear we came out of the same womb, and we may look exactly alike, but we couldn't be more different. She's wild and carefree; I'm uptight and according to my sisters when they want to get under my skin—rigid. I can't help it if I'm a planner.

"Jax made a point to challenge me in dressing casual—as if he doesn't think I can do it. Can you believe that?"

"Ha, I like this guy already. Tell me more." My sister picks up an emerald-green V-neck tee and demands, "Try this. It will make your eyes pop."

"Anyway, he's a musician. I met him at open mic night. He's really good. I think you'd like him. He plays just about everything, though I like his own music best. He's got this vibe that makes crowds go wild."

"Hmmm...." My sister's got more to say, I can tell from that tone alone, but instead of speaking her mind, she shoves my favorite pair of jeans into my hands. They fit me like they were tailor-made yet are stretchy enough so I can do just about anything in them.

Slipping both items on, I stand in front of my full-length mirror.

Not bad. Looking at my bare feet, I ask, "Shoes?"

"Will you be on the beach or somewhere in town?"

My voice raises three octaves. "Like I'd know. The rat-bastard didn't tell me anything—but casual."

Giving me a knowing smirk, she raises a brow. "So now he's a rat-bastard?"

"He's only a rat-bastard because he's made it his mission for some reason to make me unplug. He thinks I work too much and need a break."

"Hmmm... The nerve of him... yet you still agreed to go out with him."

"It's not like that... we're just friends," I quickly protest. I truly don't want her to get the wrong idea. "I've only been hanging out with him because I'm certain he's just what we're looking for in terms of finding local talent for the festival."

I ignore her blatant glance at the pile of clothes on my bed. "Okay, Sloane. You let me know how that goes."

I should know better than to lie to her, but hell... I don't even know what to make of Jax Cartwright. I mean... sure, he's kind, smart, and sexy as sin, but that doesn't mean there's anything going on between us. He's also a bossy know-it-all, who thinks he's got me pegged.

I must be lost in my head too long for Raven; the next thing I know, Raven's about to exit my room but stops to glance over her shoulder and say, "Look, Sloane... Go... have fun... and do all the things I would do..."

With that, she leaves me here with my jaw hanging to the floor.

I know exactly what my sister would do—and I'm not sure I'm ready for *that* much fun.

Chapter 9
Jax

At exactly six, I walk up the steps to Sloane's house. I've parked on the street, and I've timed it so I wouldn't be too early or one minute late. Knowing she'll still consider this tardy, I'm hoping she'll give me a pass as I wanted to give her as much time as she needs to be ready.

After two raps on the door, it swings open, and my breath catches in my throat as I take Sloane in. Standing there in an emerald-green V-neck tee that shows just a peek of cleavage has me semi-hard in an instant. It's not indecent by any means, but it shows off the curves she's been hiding under those flowy blouses she wears.

My eyes trail down her curves past her shirt tucked into well-fitting jeans.

Before I have a chance to think about saying anything, she puts up a finger and says, "Hey... give me a sec to grab my purse." With that, she turns, and the view just keeps getting better.

Her tight, round ass sways rhythmically over to where a small bag sits on a table. I swear, those jeans were made for her, and only her. They fit better than a second skin and accentuate her every curve perfectly.

When she returns, a smile plays across her face. "See... no computer... no work, just my phone and wallet. This good enough for you?"

Nodding, I grin in return. "That sounds just about right. Promise not to check emails from your phone?"

Rolling her eyes, she smirks. "I'll give you a few hours. But I can't make promises beyond that." Turning to punch in a code so the door locks, I can hear the smile in her voice. "You can't expect me to quit cold turkey. It's rare I take an entire night off."

"I can see I've got my work cut out for me." I pretend to grumble as I open the door of my truck for her.

My truck is slightly lifted, but Sloane uses the running boards like a pro and enters with ease. Once she's settled, I close the door and walk around to join her in the cab.

After I pull away from the curb, I make small talk to break the silence. It's comfortable, but I want to make the most of this time to get to know her better. I get the feeling it's a rare sight to see this side of her, and I'm not foolish enough to waste a moment of it.

"What did you end up doing today?" I ask, turning right at the stop sign.

"I spent most of the day doing some back-end things for the festival. I made graphics, updated the schedule, and all sorts of things you'd rather not hear about if you really want me to unplug."

"Point taken," comes out on a laugh. "I assume you spent most of the day working. Tell me what's something you only do for you? A guilty pleasure of sorts."

"Hmmm... that's actually harder than it should be to answer. Besides hanging with my sisters, I don't do a lot for just me. I've been so focused on school and now work. Raven and I do pedicures regularly. I also love reading at night before bed."

"What types of books do you enjoy?" I ask with interest. "Fiction or nonfiction?"

Gasping, she lets out an adorable laugh. "I guess I do have a guilty pleasure after all. Hmmm... If I'm reading, I need to escape. I've had enough of facts and statistics in school. I want all the romance. I love spicy rom-coms, as well as stories that tear my heart out and make me feel all the feels, then put it back together again. An HEA is a must."

Holy shit. So much to unpack from that. I followed most of it, but still ask for clarification, "HEA?"

"Happily ever after. Don't get me wrong, I like women's fiction and chick-lit, but give me a good ole romance, and I'll devour it."

"So... the classics?" I ask, completely out of my element.

From the corner of my eye, I watch her nose scrunch. "Don't get me wrong, I like some, but contemporary is more my jam. My sister Lanie was always reading growing up. She'd no sooner finish a book, mention its title, and I would finish it within a day or two."

"Were you always so competitive?"

"My sisters emphatically would say yes. Being one of four girls, I wanted to forge my own path, so my competitive side formed early."

That totally fits my impression of her. "Are either of your parents competitive like you?"

"Dad is probably more competitive than Mom. As a pararescue pilot, he's got to be at the top of his game. He can't afford to make mistakes—literally. But Mom's a traveling nurse, so she's good at what she does, too."

"Was she always a traveling nurse?" I probe, completely fascinated by their family dynamics.

"No. We basically stayed in University Place after my parents' divorce. When Dad got stationed at Lewis-McChord, Mom took the opportunity to be a traveling nurse. This way Lizzy could graduate where she started school, and everyone was happy."

"Did you see your dad often growing up?"

"As often as we could. He'd come to visit as much as possible and either Mom or Nana took us to see him on our breaks from school when he couldn't come to us. It certainly wasn't easy, but we've made it work."

Sighing heavily, she shrugs as if it's completely her normal. Then she adds, "It's probably why I'm so close to my sisters. We were more or less the solid unit, and our grown-ups fit the best they could into our schedules. Everyone made us a priority, so it worked."

As we drive into Cannon Beach, I pull off the highway and head into town. I'm honestly surprised Sloane hasn't peppered me with questions about our plans. Instead of going into the touristy area, I veer off and head to my favorite out of the way restaurant. It's a little mom-and-pop place that still gets some tourists, but usually, it's where the locals go if they want a night off from cooking.

When I pull up to the curb alongside the restaurant, Sloane's eyes light up. "We're going to Meg's?"

"If you're okay with it. Hang on, I'll grab your door."

Glancing to see if there's any traffic behind me, I quickly hop out and rush around the back of my truck to open her door. Thankfully, she waits for me to help her out. I know she's perfectly capable of opening it herself, but hopefully, she'll realize she'll never need to if I'm around.

The moment the door swings open, she gushes, "This is one of my favorite places. They have the best French dip sandwiches ever. Nana used to take us here. Gosh, I don't think I've been here in a few years."

"It's one of my favorites, too." I grin, holding the door to the restaurant open for her.

As Sloane walks past, she whispers, "Thank you."

The hostess greets us as soon as we enter, and we're seated immediately. Even though I'm fairly certain we both know what we want, we take a few minutes to look over the menu.

Once our drinks and food have been ordered, Sloane leans forward with her forearms against the table and smiles. "In case I forget, thanks so much for bringing me here. This place was really special to Nana. It makes me both happy and sad to be here. I cherish the memories, but I miss her, too."

"Tell me about Nana. What was she like?"

Sloane's eyes get a little misty, but at the same time, a smile forms on her face. "She was the best. She loved us so hard. She's what made things work for our family when my parents' marriage ended. She was kind, loving, and the fiercest person you'd ever meet if you wronged any of us girls.

"She was the kind of grandma you see in the movies. She always let us bake cookies and do art projects, keeping us girls out of trouble. She loved to play cards and taught us everything from *Pinochle* to *Speed*. She'd beat the pants off you in an instant. Unlike other grandmas, you had to earn the winning title; it would never be handed to you freely. Ha... maybe that's how I got to be so competitive?"

"She sounds like an amazing woman. I'm sorry I never got the chance to meet her."

Wistfully, Sloane sucks in a deep breath and slowly exhales. "Yeah, she was more than awesome. There's not a day that goes by that I don't think of her. She was one of the wittiest women I've ever met. She had these one-liners that always kept you on your toes.

"But enough about me. I've been monopolizing the conversation the entire night."

We spend the rest of dinner talking about what it was like for me to live here growing up. I laugh so hard when her eyes nearly bug out of her head during my story about how I used to bike to Cannon Beach all the time as a teenager. When I remind her it was less than ten miles, she still can't believe my parents allowed such a thing.

Afterward, we drive over to Haystack Rock. Since it's such a beautiful and warm night, we end up walking along the beach. There's about an hour until sunset, but I honestly don't think I'll notice it with Sloane next to me. She completely captivates me in every way possible.

We keep our conversation light as we walk along tide pools, steering clear of anything that will get us wet. Both of us have taken the precaution of rolling up our jeans, as we carry our socks and shoes. Neither of us want an unexpected dip in the ocean tonight.

Eventually, we find a log that's been dried out to sit on. With the light breeze blowing her hair around, Sloane must get tired of it because the next thing I know, she's got her hair tied up in a messy knot on top of her head. Seeing her shoulders relax without a worry on her face lets me know my plan is working. I don't think there's a side to Sloane that isn't sexy but watching her relax with a carefree smile on her face just might be what I like best about her. She's not worried about putting on a show or managing her list of tasks. If I had to guess, I'd say this is the side of her she rarely lets others in on —and I'm honored she feels comfortable enough to let me in.

"Oh, I talked with Ryan today. Do you mind slipping that song into your set Thursday night?"

"Is Lanie working Thursday?" I ask, wondering what his plan is.

"Nope. He wants her all to himself." She chuckles. "Though that's relative since the place will be busy—but he plans to take her there for their anniversary dinner. She won't have a clue."

"That's a solid plan. Have you figured out how to get your sisters there?"

Grinning, she rolls her eyes. "Yep. They'll be there to check out you."

"What?" I ask in disbelief. "Why me?"

"Well, Ryan is only taking Lanie to dinner, but he doesn't want my sisters to miss out on his proposal. You're the perfect cover—no pun intended."

"Well, I'm happy to be of service. Does this mean I'll finally get to meet the rest of the Lancasters? Will either of your parents make it?"

"I won't have a choice with you meeting my sisters," she says on a laugh, then grimaces. "Unfortunately, Dad's doing maneuvers in California, and Mom's taking care of a woman in Vermont, so we'll celebrate with them later."

"Is there something wrong with me meeting your sisters?"

"No... other than the fact they can be a total pain in the ass. We're a force to be reckoned with when we're together—so be warned."

I laugh at the stone-cold expression on her face. "I can't wait. I'll be sure to put on a good show for them."

"Speaking of performing... have you ever considered trying out for the Seaside Music Festival competition?"

I'm sure my eyes are wide as saucers by this sudden shift in subject. I swear my tongue nearly sticks to the roof of my mouth, but somehow, I manage to ask, "As in the one that requires performing in front of thousands of people?"

"Uh... I don't know how many people will be there, but that

sounds about right. The crowd loves you, and I think you'd be a great addition in terms of local talent."

Holy shit. Is she serious?

There's no way I'd be able to get up on stage with that many people.

She prattles on about something, but I'm no longer listening. I'm still stuck on the idea of performing in front of thousands. Hell, I just started in front of a live audience. How the hell does she think I'd be ready for a stage that big?

She finally regains my attention by waving a hand in front of my face and calling my name, "Jax? Did you hear what I just said?"

"Uh... no, I guess I didn't," I sputter. "Can you repeat that?"

"I said Smashing Waves Records is offering recording contracts to the top contestants in each category. This could be huge for you!"

Thank God I'm sitting down. First, she tells me there will be thousands of people watching; the next, she shares that a recording contract could be on the line.

Holy fucking shit, is she for real?

Tilting her head to the side, she scrutinizes my face. I have no idea what she sees, but suddenly, she gushes out, "What's going on in that head of yours, Jax? You've always got something to say."

"I... uh..." Shit, I can't even find words. Clearing the huge lump in my throat, I finally manage, "I've barely begun performing for live audiences... and you want me to go from zero to ninety in a nano-second? Why on earth do you think I could compete at that level?"

Reaching for the phone in her pocket, she says, "You surely don't see yourself clearly. Let me show you what the world sees when you perform. You could light the world on fire with the amount of energy you bring to each performance."

She taps at her screen for a moment, then turns it toward me. "This was your first performance."

Even I can clearly see how nervous I was during open mic night. My voice quavered in my introduction, and I vividly remember wanting to get the hell out of there after it was over.

"Now watch this." It's a shot of last night's performance. It's evident between the two that I'm no longer nervous. I'm singing right into the camera, which of course I was because I was singing to her. After a few more beats, my jaw drops as I watch.

If I didn't know better, I'd say this video looks like one of those clips you'd find on your favorite social media app from a fan taken of a famous rock star. The guy in the video is living it up on stage. He's got charisma and knows just how to play the crowd—which is going wild for a song I've written. They join in when I hit the chorus a second time.

"You must be one hell of an editor," I mumble. I feel like I'm having an out-of-body experience. There's no way I'm this guy.

"I'm good, but you gave me great material to work with. Look at yourself through my eyes. You have what it takes to give everyone some steep competition."

"But it's in front of a small crowd at a local bar. The competition will have thousands of people— and it's live. Not to mention all those that will watch it being recorded."

Reaching for my hand, she gives it a squeeze. "What are you so afraid of?"

"Besides making a fool of myself?" I flippantly remark because my brain just can't process what she's suggesting.

"You won't make a fool of yourself," she assures me.

"Look, Sloane, I'm great in a *small—local—bar*." I stress each word for emphasis. "What makes you think I can perform at the caliber needed to even make it beyond the initial audition?"

Wincing, she shrinks into herself, then quietly admits, "What if I told you, you already have?"

"What do you mean?" I demand.

"I've been sending these clips to Tara after I've got the edited versions. She thinks you're brilliant by the way. But she's also passed them on to the other judges, and they'd love to see you move onto the live portion of the competition."

What. The. Actual. Fuck?

Chapter 10
Sloane

Okay. Maybe he's not ready for this. The way he practically needs a shovel to get his jaw off the ground should've been my first clue. But he's got to know how good he is, right? I mean, I've been telling him this from the beginning. Does he really not believe me, or is there something else going on?

"I seriously think you'd blow the competition away, Jax."

"I... You..." he sputters but stops and clamps his mouth shut into a straight line. I usually consider myself an excellent reader of the room, but in this moment, he's got the face of a professional poker player, and I don't have a clue what's going on in that brain of his.

"Please tell me what you're thinking," I practically beg, needing to be put out of my misery.

"I don't know what to think. I knew you were showing those clips to your boss, but... hell... I never thought it would go anywhere. I'm from a Podunk town and barely have a following on social media. I've never posted a single performance, so I had no idea what others would think of my music... you know I have very little experience on stage."

He's quiet for a moment, then practically shouts, "Wait... you're telling me... I've already gotten through the first round?"

"Of course, it's completely up to you to continue," I assure him because I can't quite tell if he's angry or just in shock. "But yeah. You'll be in the lineup to perform at the festival."

Shaking his head, he mutters, "Holy shit. Is this really happening?"

"It is... if you want it," I remind him. I may be part of the biggest record label in the world, and I'm certain I can promote the shit out of him. But he's got to want this for himself, or it's a moot point.

This man is suddenly like a steel trap when it comes to sharing his thoughts.

Standing, he paces a path in front of me, from the left to the right, with his fingers steepled over his jaw. He takes about eight strides, pivots, and returns in the opposite direction. I'm quiet as I let him process everything. Though if I weren't on pins and needles waiting for his reaction, I'd probably find it comical.

My gut has never been wrong when it comes to finding talent. Jax has what it takes. I can feel it so deep in my bones, it hurts. Maybe if he tells me what's holding him back, I can help him through this?

As I wait for him to talk, my heart pounds in my chest. I truly hope I haven't upset him by taking the initiative to enter him into the competition. I thought I made that clear to him the first night we spoke.

Finally, he stops and pins me with a stare, as his hands move to his hips. His voice is thick with emotion as he demands, "Tell me, Sloane, have you ever been so excited and scared to death that you literally can't make a decision to save your life?"

"Uh..." I take a moment to think through my response. I

answer in the most honest way I can. "I've been scared... yes... but I'm not sure I've experienced what you're describing."

"Ha... That's probably true. I can't imagine you scared of anything. Could you get on stage and sing in front of thousands though?"

"Uh, I find musical talent. Not make it... trust me... I can barely carry a tune in a bucket. So, my answer is no. I couldn't. But that's not to say I couldn't get on that stage and talk or introduce acts. Crowds don't scare me. Put me somewhere up high and unprotected, and I'd be shaking like a leaf. We all have fears, Jax—it doesn't mean we can't conquer them."

Crossing his arms over his chest, he looks down at me. "You make it sound so easy."

"I'm sure it's easier said than done. But talk to me. Tell me what's bothering you most, and I can help you find a way to work through this."

Shaking his head, he exhales heavily. "I'm not even sure what's wrong. First, I'm in shock. I can't believe I've already made it through the first round. But mostly, I'm terrified I'll get onto that big stage and choke or fall off or do something that will go viral, and I'll be the laughingstock of the world."

"Has any of those things ever happened in the past?" I ask, wondering if this has triggered some childhood trauma or something.

Huffing out a quick breath, he grunts, "No... but who's to say it couldn't?"

"What would you say if I could work my magic and build up some hype for your music? Let's release some of these clips onto social media, and you can see for yourself how fans react."

When he doesn't readily respond, I quickly add, "We can also work on getting you to perform in some bigger venues. We've got a few weeks before the competition. You can use working at Pop's to build your set list. You saw how the crowd of strangers loves your music already. I'm certain everyone else will, too."

Hesitantly, he asks, "And... I don't have to decide today?"

"Not at all." He watches as I pull up my go-to app for Smashing Waves Records and ask, "What's your handle? I want to tag you in this. That way you can see for yourself just how much fans will love you."

He briefly tells me, and it's almost too good to be true in terms of name recognition. The man used his full name and not some crazy nickname with a zillion numbers or something abstract. It's something I would've hand-picked for him if I could. After a few clicks and selecting the perfect hashtags, I look to him and ask, "You ready for this?"

Letting out a deep breath as if he's been holding the weight of the world, I see his shoulders finally relax. "There's only one way to know... go for it."

To maximize his exposure, I switch media apps and go through the same process a few more times. Once I've posted everywhere I normally do when I'm trying to get all eyes on a client, I look up to him with a grin. "Done."

"Now what do we do?" he sighs, plopping down beside me.

Reaching for his hand to calm his nerves, I give it a squeeze. "We sit back, enjoy this sunset, and wait."

Chapter 11
Jax

It's barely six in the morning, and my phone won't stop pinging with notifications. I tossed and turned for hours after dropping Sloane off at her house, and I'm too damn tired to get out of bed just yet. For some dumbass reason, I've got my phone plugged in and resting on my dresser—a trick I use to make myself get out of bed to turn off my alarm in the morning. I don't have to work until two, and I don't have any alarms set, so who the hell is blowing up my phone at this hour?

When my phone buzzes again, I groan in frustration and drag myself from my bed. Trudging to my dresser, I grab the phone and throw myself back under the covers of my bed.

I'd planned to turn it off and go back to sleep, but curiosity gets the better of me. I type in my passcode, and of course, I get it wrong the first time—damn thick fingers. But my screen opens on the second try.

I open the offending app that's keeping me from sleep, and I can't believe my eyes. Rubbing them to make sure they're working properly, I blink rapidly and look again.

I have 5,369 notifications from this app alone.

"Holy. Fucking. Shit. This can't be happening."

Wondering if I just got spammed by the bots, I click on the first notification, and I'm immediately brought to the video Sloane posted. I don't bother watching it, but my eyes bug out of their sockets when I see the number of views this video has in less than twenty-four hours.

"Two point six million views. Are you fucking kidding me?"

My fingers tremble, and I can barely hold my phone in place. Glutton for punishment, I squeeze my eyes shut and mentally prepare for the onslaught of comments. I'm certain there will be some trolls, but I have no idea how many. When I feel I can handle whatever's hiding in the comment thread, I open my eyes and slowly press the link.

The first comment reads:

"I need to see this LIVE! When and where?"

As I scroll through, many comments are similar. Most like my music and can't wait to see more. A couple are from people I know, and I'm wondering how this ended up on their FYP, while most are from complete strangers. I'm overwhelmed and in utter shock from the amount of responses. I had no idea one of my videos would go viral.

My cheeks burn when I come to some that are wildly inappropriate, and it takes everything in me not to reply.

No... I am not looking for a baby mama. I'm not looking for someone to lick me from head to toe either... and I'm certainly not interested in a three-way because both her and her husband think I'm hot.

The nerve of some people.

Thankfully, those comments are few and far between. I

continue reading the words, but my brain can't fathom this reality. This is next-level insanity.

Just as I'm about to put my phone away, I'm tagged in another video from Sloane. Clicking it open, I wonder if this woman ever sleeps. To my surprise, this one is me interacting with the crowd between songs. Then I close my eyes and start into one of my favorite songs I've written to date—"Hoping You See This." It's one I wrote about feeling invisible when it comes to a childhood crush. It's not about anyone specifically, rather a fictitious girl I'd hopefully meet some day, and she'd feel what I'm feeling for her. I wrote it after I watched my roommate start dating, and I was stuck alone in our apartment each night.

Knowing she's up, I tap out a text to Sloane.

Me: Holy shit. Is this really happening?

Immediately, her response comes through.

Sloane: You'd better get used to it. I told you you'd be a hit.

Me: Over two million views??? How the hell could I even fathom that.

Sloane: Have you been brave enough to look through the comments?

Me: Not all 5000 of them. But enough to get the point.

Sloane: And that is???

Me: That people like my music

Sloane: Did you think I've been lying to you?

> Me: No. But it doesn't mean I was prepared for this either.

> Sloane: I've got an early meeting online. I've gotta run. Live it up, Rock Star! This is only the beginning for you… mark my words.

> Me: I'm not sure to be excited or terrified that you've set your mind to this. Have a good day.

> Sloane: Be afraid… Very afraid (rubs palms together). I've got big plans for you. Talk soon.

Laughing, I silence my app notifications and throw my phone on my bed beside me. I need to get some sleep if I'm going to work until ten tonight.

Just as I'm about to drift off, my phone rings with a call from my sister. She's in the same house as me, so what the hell is she calling me for at this hour?

"I'm literally right down the hall from you. Why are you calling?" I say in greeting. I know I'm an ass, but it's annoying when she could literally walk down the hall to tell me what she needs.

"I didn't know if you were home," Emily admits.

"There's this thing called knocking on my door, or I don't know, looking to see if my truck is in the driveway."

All I get is a huff of irritation through the phone.

"Was there a point to you calling so early?"

I hear movement on the other end, then a knock at my door. "Come in!" I holler when I realize she's hung up.

Emily's got her hair stacked into a messy bun and is wearing a pair of sleep pants and an oversized hoodie. Something must be important if she's up this early.

Sitting up, I ask, "What's up?"

She stares at me for the longest time, then she asks, "Do you know you're trending?"

Nodding, I admit, "Crazy, isn't it?"

"You could've clued me in. Why am I the last to know you're a freaking rock star?"

Running a hand down my face, I counter, "I wouldn't go so far as saying that. I'm not a rock star by any means. I've simply played a few sets."

She looks at me as if I'm stupid or something. "Jax... Smashing Waves Records is posting your performance on their website and all social media apps. Do you have some secret life in college that you haven't made us privy to?"

"Not at all." I quickly explain how Dad heard me playing one day and challenged me to take my shot, so I went to open mic. I told her how Sloane saw me that first night and got me a regular gig at Pop's Hops.

"I had no idea people would respond this way to my music."

Her eyes widen slightly, and she uses her hands to emphasize her thoughts. "Have you seen how *big* that video's blown up?"

"Again. I wasn't expecting that. Sloane did it to prove a point last night."

"What point was she trying to make?" my sister counters.

"She thinks I should join the Seaside Music Festival competition. Can you believe that?"

"The bigger question is, why can't you? You're obviously killing it on stage. She's posted two videos of you and from what I've seen, she's got a point. You're good."

"Thanks." Glancing at the clock, I wonder aloud, "What are you doing up so early?"

"Well... for starters, Mom and Dad are coming home later

today, and I need to finish my chores. I also crashed early last night and woke up this morning to see my brother of all people is trending on my FYP. A few of my friends have already reached out to see if it's really you."

"Well, it's me. Try not to make that big of a deal about it. I'm still the same older brother you've been living with your entire life. Trends fade. I'm sure I will, too."

"When exactly are you performing? I'd love to see you in person."

"I plan to invite Mom and Dad to Pop's Hops when they return. With the new remodel, there's an outdoor seating area minors can be in. You're welcome to come anytime."

"I think I'll check it out. By the way, I'm heading out to get some coffee; want me to pick you up anything?" she offers.

"Nah, I'm good. I'm going back to sleep for a bit since I don't work until later today. I slept for shit last night, and I won't make it through my shift today if I don't."

Chapter 12
Sloane

I haven't seen Jax since I sprung the competition on him. Between him working nights, his parents back in town, and my schedule looking for more local talent, it just hasn't worked out. So far, I've posted three videos in the past few days that have each skyrocketed further than the last, as far as trending goes.

I knew people would like his music, but even I wasn't prepared for the level of success he attains. I've got about six more videos ready to go and thankfully, tonight, I'll be able to get footage to make more.

With Jax's sudden popularity, I've managed to invite Raven and Lizzy with ease to Pop's, and they're totally in the dark about Ryan's proposal. We're meeting after six, and Jax will play from seven until nine-thirty. I'm not exactly sure Ryan's plan, but I can't wait to see it unfold. Based on recent social media posts, I'm sure the place will be packed. Apparently, Ryan's arranged with Joe, to get a reserved table next to the dance floor, so I chose one where we can watch the action. Usually, Joe doesn't reserve tables, but he's seen the trending videos and expects a crowd. He also wants to make the night as special for Lanie in any way he can.

To pass the time while I wait for my siblings, I pull out my laptop and finish some work I'd planned to do later tonight. I'm knee deep in my tasks when the hairs on the back of my neck tingle. Glancing around, I spot Jax parking his truck across the street. I can't help but smile at my traitorous reaction to him. Closing my laptop, so he won't think I'm a complete workaholic, I watch as he grabs his guitar from the back of his truck and saunters across the street.

He's got the total musician vibe going for him. My mouth waters as I take in his tight, fitted black t-shirt that accentuates his broad shoulders and muscled chest. Damn, those corded arms. He must get those from playing so much. I'm dying to know what it would feel like to have them wrap around me. His well-worn, perfectly fitting jeans and black boots round out his outfit to perfection.

I can tell the moment he spots me because his face splits into a grin, causing my belly to swirl with excitement. There's something different about him tonight and as he steps closer to me, it hits me—his face is free of scruff. I like scruffy Jax, but clean shaven totally works, too. I wouldn't kick either of them out of bed for eating crackers. Suddenly, I want to run my tongue along that chiseled jaw and kiss the living hell out of him.

When a car passes between us, breaking our connection, I'm brought back to my senses.

Where the hell did that come from?

Geez, Sloane. Get it together. You shouldn't think about him like that. You're helping him win this competition—and that's it. Besides, even though he's been a closet musician, he's still a musician—and that has heartache written all over it. Especially with the way he looks as if he wants to devour me in this moment. I know I'm not imagining whatever this is between us. The tension with Jax is thicker than I've ever experienced with any man, and if I don't get my shit together before my sisters arrive, they'll see right through me.

The moment he steps up to my table, a devilish grin forms on his face. "I see you're making every second count. You don't need to stop on my account." He may like to tease, but I love that he gets me.

"I'm good. I've got what I needed done for today; the rest is just a bonus."

Pulling out a chair across from me, he sits. Then he leans forward against the table between us. "When will your sisters get here?"

"I'm not sure when Ryan and Lanie will arrive, but since he's got a table reserved, I'm assuming they'll all get here within the hour."

"Does your sister have any clue?"

Shaking my head, I grin. "Nope. As far as she's concerned, they're just celebrating their anniversary tonight. He made a point to talk it up and say something about making sure he preorders a full marionberry pie from Nell. I think they'll end up taking it to-go for a walk along the beach later. It's sort of their thing."

"Will he want the mic to propose? Or will it be something he keeps private?"

"Uh... shit... he never mentioned anything about it being public. I'm almost certain he'll keep it private. But I have no idea to be honest."

"I'll just keep my eye out and go with the flow. By the way, if you have a few minutes tonight, I'd like to introduce you to my family when they arrive. They're dying to meet the person who's made me go viral."

"Oh, Jax," I quickly dismiss. "That was all you. I'm just the person who captured it on camera."

Rolling his eyes, he mutters, "Whatever you say, Sloane."

"Hey, Jax," a girl's voice calls from the street, interrupting my thoughts.

When I glance her way, she's frantically waving in our direction. Not sure if this is someone he knows, or a newfound fan, I eye Jax warily. I'll take his lead, whatever the case.

Thankfully, his eyes light up as he pops up from the table and closes the distance between them. As I glance around, I'm surprised to see not many tables left. I must've been so caught up in my work, I didn't notice the crowd filing in.

As Jax and the girl walk to my table, they're joined with an older couple I can only assume is his parents. Their family resemblance is uncanny. They each have dark hair, strong bone structure, and a different variation of blue eyes.

The kids are the perfect combination of their parents. Emily's hair is a bit lighter in color; it's long and flows past her shoulders, the same as her mom. She's dressed in a pair of dark jeans and a gray zip-up hoodie. Though Jax is the tallest of them, his dad isn't far behind him in height.

Looking at his dad, it's like glancing into the future to see what Jax will become, especially since they're both clean shaven. The only difference is Mr. Cartwright has a lot more laugh lines and is graying at his temples.

When Mrs. Cartwright smiles, I can clearly see where Jax inherited his. It lights up the room as she gushes, "You must be Sloane. It's so nice to meet you."

As I stand to greet them, she leans in for a hug.

Let me tell you, Mrs. Cartwright may be smaller than me in stature, but she's a fierce hugger. It reminds me of Nana's, and I promptly return it with all I've got. There's nothing better than a good hug. When she releases me, I step back and say, "It's so nice to meet all of you. I'm glad you could make it. You're in for a treat tonight. Jax keeps getting better with each performance."

Shaking her head, Mrs. Cartwright looks to Jax. "I still can't believe you kept this from us for all these years. If it weren't for you going viral, I'd have never known your talent."

"Mom," Jax admonishes. "I told you... none of this was planned or meant to be kept from you. It all just happened."

"I'm so proud of you, son. I, for one, can't wait to see you in front of a crowd," his dad says as he pats Jax on the shoulder.

"Thanks, Dad. It should be quite the show." Leaning in so that only his parents and I can hear, he whispers, "I've been asked to play a song so Ryan Murdock can propose tonight."

"Oh my." Mrs. Cartwright looks around. "Will his parents be here?"

Jax looks to me, to which I reply, "I have no idea."

"Well then, I'd better have my camera at the ready so I can send it to his mom. We're in the same book club."

Sometimes I forget how small this town can be—what are the odds?

"Mom," Jax suddenly blurts in warning. "Don't you dare say anything until it happens—and then let them be the first to announce it. Even Sloane's sisters are in the dark, and I'm not ruining Ryan's surprise."

When his mom cocks her head to the side with confusion clearly written all over her features, Jax quickly adds, "Ryan's proposing to Sloane's sister Lanie. It's a long story. But don't say a word... here they come."

Sure enough, Ryan's leading Lanie through the crowd to the table.

"This is so exciting!" Jax's sister quietly claps her hands together but stops when Jax pointedly glares at her.

Before anyone can say another word, Mr. Cartwright pats

me on the shoulder. "It was nice meeting you, Sloane, but we'd better grab a table if we want to get a good view." He winks at his wife, then points at a table near Lanie. "Let's take that one."

"Oh, good idea, honey," Mrs. Cartwright agrees, then says to me, "It was nice meeting you, sweetie. I hope we see more of you."

"Mom..." comes from Jax on a moan as his sister giggles.

God, I love this family. They are a riot.

The moment they leave, Jax points his thumb to the stage behind him. "I'd better get things set up." He turns, then stops to pin me with his beautiful blue eyes. "Hey, before you leave tonight, I'd like to discuss something with you."

"What's that?"

His sexy lips spread into a smirk. "You'll find out soon enough."

With that, he turns on a dime, walks to the stage, and gets ready to play, leaving me completely wanting more than just the answer to my question.

Chapter 13
Jax

I know I'm an ass for leaving things like that—but what I have to say to Sloane is best without an audience. It will also take more time than I've got before I'm due on stage. As I make my way through the crowd, I'm surprised to see so many people for a Thursday night. Glancing into the bar through the under-cover area, the place is packed.

Is there an event in town I didn't know about? Or are all these people here to see me? Shit—I don't know, but I can't think about that now. I need to focus.

By the time I introduce myself to the crowd, there isn't a seat left onsite. One thing I love about this venue is I can perform no matter the weather. When Joe remodeled, he had it designed so an entire wall opens to the outside with an adjoining outdoor covered patio. The stage is built so it can be inside the building in the winter and open to the outside during the summer. Since we are a coastal town in the Pacific North-west, heaters are built into the ceiling, so patrons won't get cold.

I know everyone is here for the music, so I keep my

speaking to a minimum. "I'm Jax Cartwright. Thanks for coming out tonight. Are you ready for some fun?"

From the loud cheers that erupt, they are clearly ready. "Before I begin, I want to say a special thanks to my dad. He may not know it, but his support and encouragement is a big part of why I'm on stage with you tonight." I take a moment to meet his gaze and continue, "I hope you enjoy the show."

Strumming a few chords, I check to see if my guitar is in tune, and I launch into my version of his favorite song—"American Pie." In my few short weeks of playing on stage, I've quickly learned if I start out with a crowd favorite, they are far more engaged when I sprinkle in my own songs.

As I sing, my heart soars when I catch glimpses of my parents' expressions. In an instant, I can tell they're both equally in shock and proud. It makes me realize how ridiculous it was to keep this to myself. It wasn't that I purposely kept my music as a secret, it just never occurred to me that others would want to hear it.

Obviously, I was wrong—if the crowd's reaction to this song ending is anything to go by. I'm not sure what I'd been so worried about. As I transition into another cover song, this time by Shawn Mendes, I realize I'd been a fool. I love performing and now that I'm over my initial fear, I know this is something that isn't going away.

Glancing to Sloane, I see she's still sitting alone. Hopefully, her sisters will arrive soon, so Ryan won't have to wait too much longer. I made a point to text her my set list, so she could pass it along to him, and he'll know approximately when he can make his move. But if her sisters aren't here, I'll be flexible. There's no way I could let them miss this.

I can't imagine what Ryan's feeling in this moment. I'm sure that ring is burning a hole in his pocket, waiting for the right time. I'd be like a cat jumping across a hot tin roof—

nothing but a bundle of nerves until I was able to finally pop the question. Ryan is a saint to sit there so cool and collected.

There's no way I could do that.

As I launch into the original cover of "You're Beautiful" by James Blunt, my eyes are once again drawn to Sloane. Couples from around the room get up to dance. People sway between us, but my eyes never leave hers. God, she's gorgeous. Her smile is hypnotic, and I'm completely in a trance as the words flow through me melodically.

It's uncanny the parallels of how my life are to this song. Here I am singing about meeting a beautiful girl. Unlike the words go in the song, I'm not sure I'm worthy of her, but I want to take my shot. The more I get to know her, the more I like her. She's not only beautiful, but she's smart, funny, and competitive as hell. I certainly hope that will play to my advantage later tonight. God only knows how this woman will react.

When the song ends, I notice two girls slip into the seats next to Sloane. As I break into my next song, I find myself needing to close my eyes so I can concentrate on the words. I just wrote this song a few weeks ago, and I want to make it perfect.

It's about taking chances, never giving up, and the courage to believe in yourself. It talks specifically of my journey of getting to this place. It makes me feel raw, and I know if I look at anyone I know, I might not be able to get through it. It's a lot more upbeat than "You're Beautiful" so when I open my eyes during the chorus, I'm pleased to find people still on the dance floor. By the end of the second verse, I'm surprised to find many are singing the chorus as they dance to the beat.

Their energy flows through me, and I take things up a notch. Leaving my entire heart on the line, I slide through the third verse with ease. By the time I hit the last note, I know I've given it my all. The feedback from the room is deafening, and it takes a while for them to settle down. I take this time to risk glancing at my family. Emily is on her feet screaming while my parents remain seated. Mom's blotting her eyes with a napkin, while Dad's nodding at me. Even though he doesn't say a word, his message is clear. *I knew you could do this. I'm so proud of you.*

As the crowd settles, I make eye contact with Ryan, lifting only a brow to see if he's ready. When he gives me a slow nod as he wraps his arm around Lanie, I take my cue and lean into the mic.

"Ladies and gentlemen, I've got a special request tonight. I hope you all enjoy my version of "Thinking Out Loud," originally by Ed Sheeran."

As if on cue, Lanie squeals and drags Ryan the few feet to the dance floor.

She has no idea just how memorable this song will be.

Chapter 14
Sloane

Lanie couldn't play more into Ryan's plan if she tried. I've already had my camera rolling because Jax killed that last song. I was almost in tears when I scanned the room and got a shot of his parents' reaction to his performance. The love they have for their son can be felt bone deep.

My view from this angle captures both Jax on stage and my sister dancing. Ryan must know I'm recording, or a miracle is happening in this moment because I'm able to capture him clearly singing the words directly to Lanie. He doesn't just sway to the music like most are around them. No, he's leading Lanie around the dance floor like a boss. He never breaks eye contact with her as he sings about how he's found love and no matter how old they get, he'll always love her.

When the musical solo hits, he spins Lanie out and twirls her around, pulling her back in time for the words to return, so he can sing into her ear. For the remainder of the song, he holds her close, never letting go. Even from here, their love is tangible and felt throughout every inch of my body.

I could only hope to find a love like that.

Goose bumps spread down my spine in anticipation, as the song comes to an end. I risk glancing away to ensure Raven and Lizzy are watching this, too. Once I have their attention, I point to Lanie and silently demand, "Watch."

When Jax finishes the song, the room bursts into applause. But Jax motions for them to quiet down and slowly the noise lowers as people look around, wondering what's happening. Ryan and Lanie are none the wiser as Jax gives the universal *shhh* sign, by placing his finger over his mouth and points to the adorable couple deep in conversation.

Since I'm not too far away, I'm able to hear Ryan clearly. "Lanie, one year ago this week, I barged into your life. I know your initial thought was that the *Texas Chainsaw Massacre* were attacking you..." Laughter erupts from around them, and Jax steps closer with the mic, keeping the couple completely unaware of his presence, yet suddenly, we're able to hear once again.

"I never had the privilege of meeting Jane Lancaster, but she set things in motion that somehow brought me to you." Just the mention of Nana's name has my heart clenching as tears sting my eyes. Blinking a few times, I notice Lanie's doing the same.

"Within a few weeks, I knew without a doubt, you were it for me. Between your smile, heart, and drive for living, I fell for you more each day. This last year together at school has only solidified my feelings for you. You get every part of me. You challenge me to be the best version of myself, and you have the most beautiful heart. Like the song Jax just performed, I know without a doubt, I want to spend the rest of my life with you. I want to love you until we're way past seventy and beyond."

My heart squeezes tight as Lanie's hands fly to her mouth, knowing what's next.

Ryan drops to one knee and pulls out a small dark box from

his pocket. His strong voice never wavers as he looks adoringly into her eyes. As he lifts the box toward her, it opens. "Melanie Lancaster, if I promise to fall more in love with you each day, will you marry me?"

I watch through watery eyes as my sister nods profusely. Then she throws herself into his arms as she squeals, "Yes. Ohmigod...Yes... Ryan... I love you so much."

Her lips crash onto his, and Ryan kisses her as if they're the only two in the room.

The place roars with hoots and hollers as Jax confirms, "She said yes! I'd love to be the first to congratulate this beautiful couple. I wish you a lifetime of love and happiness!"

Once again, the room roars with celebratory cheers, and happiness spreads everywhere.

As if he's suddenly aware everyone in the room is watching, Ryan quickly pulls Lanie to her feet. Wrapping his long arms around her, he lifts her with ease and swings her around in a circle, making her squeal with delight. Eventually, his spinning slows, and he sets her on her feet. I can't hear what is said as the crowd's absolutely going wild. But my heart melts when he runs a hand under her chin to make eye contact before sweetly kissing her.

With the box still in his hand, he pulls out the ring and slips it on her finger.

Unable to contain my excitement, I barrel over to congratulate them. My sisters must feel the same because the next thing I know, we're piling in a group hug, squeezing the hell out of one another.

When we pull apart, Raven looks to me pointedly. "Did you know about this?" She doesn't wait for an answer; she simply shakes her head as she mumbles, "Oh, why am I asking... of course you knew. You probably set this whole thing up, didn't you?"

Ryan clears his throat. "I'll have you know I actually came up with the idea—though Sloane did help in getting Jax involved."

"It was beautiful, Ryan," Lizzy says as she reaches to give him a side hug. "I couldn't be happier to call you my brother."

Reaching in, I wrap my sister in a hug. "I'm so happy for you, Lanie."

When we pull apart, she bops me on the nose. "Just how long did you know about this?"

"Awhile," I admit. "But your future husband can keep a secret. He didn't let me in on it until he needed help, and then he swore me to secrecy. I wasn't even allowed to tell Raven."

"Oh...That must've been hard," she teases. She and I both know I am the keeper of secrets in our household, even from my other half as much as it pains me.

"Thankfully, it was only for the last week or so," I admit.

Holding up her hand so we all can see her ring, she squeals. "I'm getting married."

We can barely contain our excitement as we fling our arms around one another in one long embrace.

When Jax starts into another cover by Ed Sheeran, Lanie grabs my hands. "Come on, I know you know this one." We all must line-dance. Typically, I'm working, but tonight's about my sister, so I put that thought aside and fall in line. With my sisters by my side, I let the music take over and move with the beat. This song is fast and moves me all around the floor.

As I turn and jump, now facing the stage to make my next moves in the dance, Jax captures my eyes. His eyes heat as they focus on my body swaying through the steps. God, he makes me feel sexy. I'm sure it has everything to do with the words in this song but somehow, it's like he's singing about me.

I know I must be imagining things, but I swear as he sings, he's telling me exactly what he wants. He wants to be the guy kissing me, staying up all day and night, making him shiver with the things I'd do to him.

Hell, if he keeps looking at me like that, I just might let him.

When the dance makes me jump and face the next wall, I'm forced to break eye contact. Immediately, a sense of loss flows through me but somehow, I feel the heat of his eyes, as I move through the motions for the rest of the song.

If Jax has the capacity to light me on fire from just a simple look, God only knows what he'll do to me between the sheets. Desire flows through me as I dance, and I can't help but daydream of the possibilities.

After the song ends, Lizzy leads me back to the table. "Let's get something to drink. I'm dying of thirst."

Waving down a waitress, we quickly order a Coke and wait with Raven for our drinks. Lanie and Ryan return to their meal that's now arrived, and my sisters and I watch Jax finish his performance.

They get up a few times to dance, but I remain at the table, capturing more footage of Jax. They give me shit for working all the time, but they also know what I have riding on this, so I know it's mostly them just pestering me to have fun, too.

Ryan and Lanie eventually say their goodbyes and disappear to continue their night of celebration, while Raven and Lizzy wait to finally meet Jax in person. We listen as he stacks song after song of his own work into the set. With each song he writes, he just keeps getting better. Lizzy, Raven, and I grab some dinner for ourselves while we wait.

Before stuffing a fry into her mouth, Raven asks, "So... what are your plans after this? I'm sure the happy couple is celebrating—and I'd rather give them some space."

Rolling her eyes, Lizzy shakes her head. "I'd rather not think about that—thank you very much. There's a late movie with Bradley Cooper in it. Wanna see that before heading home?"

"I'm in," Raven agrees, and they look to me.

"I... uh... think I'll stick around here for a bit. Jax said he wanted to discuss something and with the festival coming up, I'd like to tackle what he needs sooner than later."

"Oh, I'm sure you'll tackle something... or rather someone," Raven taunts. "I've seen the way that man's watched you *all night*. I'm sure he's got a lot to *talk* with you about."

Dreamily, Lizzy sighs. "It's like Lanie all over again, isn't it?"

Raven looks to Lizzy and nods. "But you know Sloane. She'll deny it until her last breath. So don't waste your time."

"Besides, she works too much. *She doesn't have time to date.*" The brat exaggerates, and Raven has the nerve to laugh.

"Um... I'm right here, *and I can hear you?*"

"Oh, poor Sloaney," Raven whines. "All work and no play makes for a dull and lonely day, don't ya think, Liz?"

"OMG—Whatever." I roll my eyes in irritation. "Once the festival is over, I won't be as busy. I'll make time for you, I promise."

Suddenly, the place fills with cheers. Hoots and hollers are all that I hear in the deafening sound. When I glance to find out what's happening on stage, I see Jax hopping off his stool and walking down the stairs. I can't believe I hadn't noticed his closing remarks.

He makes his way through the crowd to his parents first. He's stopped several times along the way with fans talking to him, but eventually, he makes it to their table. It melts my heart as I watch both his mom and sister gush over him. I can't hear what's said, but from the way Jax nods, and his dad pats him on the arm, I can tell they're happy for him. Eventually, they each hug him and say their goodbyes.

Then he turns and walks toward us. Again, he's patient with his newfound fans and for the most part, they simply say a few words and let him keep moving. When he finally reaches our table, he asks, "Mind if I join you?"

"Not at all," Lizzy gushes before I can say a word. "You were fantastic tonight. I can see what all the fuss is about."

"Uh... thanks," Jax says humbly as he looks between the three of us. When he gets to Raven, he immediately darts his eyes back to mine and widen for a fraction of a moment before he introduces himself. "I'm Jax, and you are?"

Shit. He's only met Lanie. I quickly correct my mistake. "This is my younger sister Lizzy, and that's Raven."

"Raven..." he draws out, then turns to scrutinize my features.

"Sloane, did you not mention you have a twin?" Raven says on a laugh.

"Uh... I thought I had..." I say, thinking back through our conversations.

Jax chuckles. "No... she most certainly didn't. She's talked about both of you, but I would've remembered that tidbit. I apologize for being so caught off guard."

"I'm so used to everyone already knowing. It didn't even cross my mind," I add on a laugh. "This is Raven, my other half. My partner in crime."

"Truthfully, you all have a strong family resemblance, but I wasn't expecting there to be two of you."

"We may look alike, but trust me—we're complete opposites," Raven assures him. "She's my Yin to her Yang. Sloane's got everything planned to the second, and I'm more of a go with the flow kind of gal. That's why she graduated a year early and is ditching me for the real world this fall."

"I'm not ditching you," I remind her.

"But it'll be the first time we've lived apart since the womb,

Sloaney. What will I do without you?" I know my sister's teasing, but there's a truth in what she's saying. I know that I'll miss her just as much.

I shake my head at her sudden theatrics. "Uh, I'm sure you'll survive. Stop being so dramatic. It's not like we saw much of one another this past year, even if we did live in the same apartment. We've had our own lives for years."

"True, but it doesn't mean I won't miss you."

"I hate to break this party up," Lizzy interrupts, "But if we're going to catch that movie, Raven, we've got twenty minutes until it starts."

Jumping up from the table, Raven says, "Shoot, we've got to go. Jax, it was great meeting you."

"Great job tonight, Jax," Lizzy says, standing next to Raven. To me, she says, "You okay getting yourself home?"

"I'm good. See you at the house," I say to both my sisters. Then I shoo them to the door. "Go. You're going to be late."

"It was great meeting you two," Jax calls out as my sisters rush away.

Once they're gone, he turns to me with a laugh. "Well, that was fun. You all are hilarious!"

"We have our moments—trust me," I draw out sarcastically. "So now that we're alone, what is it you wanted to talk about?"

Leaning back in his chair, he crosses his arms. "Well... I've been thinking about the competition at the festival."

Instantly, I'm all ears. Eagerly, I ask, "You're going to do it?"

"I will..." he draws out and raises a brow in challenge. "On one condition..."

I'm not sure why his expression is so smug, so I draw out, "And that is...."

"Well... If I'm facing one of my biggest fears, it's only fair... that you should, too."

Chapter 15
Sloane

What the hell have I gotten myself into?

Here I am, strapped into a five-point harness, wearing a helmet to keep me from smashing my brains to smithereens, attached to rope that's thin as hell, on a belay device designed to catch me if I fall. Sure, there are nets below me for an added safety measure, but I'm not willing to risk testing them.

Jax is strapped into his own contraption a few feet ahead of me. He's making his way across this freaking obstacle course from hell. He makes everything look so mother-fucking simple, I want to scream. If I ever catch up to the rat-bastard, I'll likely punch him in the face for even suggesting I *conquer my fears*.

He gave me the ultimatum at the bar last week, and my competitive self just had to meet his challenge. Oh, what a fool I was to think I could do this. Yes, I want him to perform at the festival. Yes, I'll go to great lengths to help him overcome his fear of performing in front of a large crowd. And yes, I want him to succeed and for the world to see his amazing talents.

Apparently, that also includes strapping myself into a freaking harness and following him through a ropes course. He thinks he's doing this to show me that I'm a strong, independent person who can conquer my biggest fear.

News flash—I still hate heights.

Well, it's not really the height. It's the falling that I'm more afraid of—well, actually landing—and the whole sudden stop thing. Yeah, I'm not a fan of that. It's not that I'm scared per se; it's more that I hate feeling out of control. I make logical and precise decisions with calculated risk daily. I'm strong and would even consider myself athletic. I work out regularly and enjoy pushing my body through new challenges.

But this ropes course just might go down as my worst decision to date.

It's bad enough that it starts a little over five feet off the ground. If I had fallen then, I'd probably be able to figure out how to tuck and roll and not injure myself permanently. But Jax had to ask if I was ready for more.

Of course, my traitorous ego kicked in, and I wasn't about to show him just how scared I was. So, when he reached for my hand, I took it and followed him up the freaking stairs to the next level, where we clipped into yet another set of obstacles. This time, we're required to walk across a swinging bridge of sorts, each step being a little swing independent of the next step.

Oh. My. Fucking. God. What the hell was I thinking?

"You've got this, Sloane. Just put one foot on the swing and use the guide ropes to propel you to the next step. I know you can do this," Jax encourages from the next landing area.

The sexy athletic God that he is, traversed this with ease just moments ago. He made it look as simple as sipping sweet tea on a hot afternoon. One, two, three, four, he swung across each step with such grace, I was in awe.

Of course, now that I'm trying to cross, the swings are still in motion and it's way freaking harder than it looked just moments ago. Clutching the rope above me with all my might, I step off the landing onto the first swing.

Forward. Back. Forward Back.

Watching the board in front of me, I find my rhythm. Throwing my weight forward, I transition onto it as it swings with me. If I can just ignore everything and only focus on the moving steps ahead of me, I think I can do this. Tuning the entire world out, I repeat this process one, two, three more times. The next thing I know, I'm being pulled into strong arms as I step onto the platform.

Jax's strong arms envelop me into a hug. "I knew you could do this. You're one of the bravest people I know. We've only got one part left at this level, then we can climb to the top and zipline down. I promise, you'll get through this."

The next part doesn't have moving pieces, though it's higher in the air. Taking my hand, Jax walks with me to the next challenge. This time, I can use two hands to hold on the entire time as I walk along a zig-zag of a balance beam. Logically, I know that if I keep three points of contact stable, I should make it across to the other side.

But it's still so freaking high.

Of course, Jax crosses it with ease. I'm sure it helps that he's so much taller than me, and he has less steps to make as he crosses the distance to the other side. When he gets to the platform, he turns and patiently waits for me to muster up the courage to cross myself.

As far as this obstacle course is concerned, this is actually one of the easier tasks. Gripping my hands on the ropes above me, I'm thankful for wearing the gloves the course provided. I can easily slide my hands along the lines running parallel above me and never have to truly loosen my grip. Below me is a board about four inches thick, just like the balance beam I used to walk on when I was younger in gymnastics. The only difference is this board isn't in a straight line.

Step by step, I make my way across the beam, zigging and zagging, never letting go of the tight rope in my hands. Keeping my breathing steady and my eyes only on the next step in front of me. This time, when I reach the platform, I'm slightly more relaxed. The only thing that's left is to climb the stairs to the last platform and zip-line down.

I can do this.

Again, Jax wordlessly takes my hand and guides me up the steps. The moment we step onto the platform, an employee takes each of our safety ropes and secures them onto the line that will bring us back to the ground. Knowing I'll need a moment to psyche myself up for this, I let him take the lead once again. Before he steps off the ledge, he leans in and whispers in my ear, "You've got this. I believe in you. I'll see you when you get down there."

And with that, he kisses me on the cheek and turns to the attendant. "I'm ready."

The attendant says, "Grab the handle and lift your legs straight out in front of you. When you get to the bottom, someone will be there to help you."

Thankfully, as I watch, Jax doesn't go as fast as I thought he would, so my nerves are put to ease a bit. When it's my turn, I think the hardest part is stepping off the platform. Thankfully, the attendant has me sit, so I know the line will hold my weight securely.

Once I step off, I shut my eyes, and it feels like I'm simply on a swing as I make my way to the ground. When my ride slows down, I allow my eyes to open, and I'm relieved to see Jax waiting for me.

The moment I'm unhooked from this contraption, I rush into his arms, squealing, "I did it!"

Lifting me, he squeezes me tight, then spins me around. I'm so high from the adrenaline rush and all things Jax in this moment, it doesn't even register when he sets me down. Then I reach up on my toes and kiss him.

Or at least I think it's me who initiates the kiss.

I really don't know.

And frankly, I don't care.

All that matters is that the weeks of pent-up tension that's been brewing between us is released as I kiss the living hell out of this man. Our lips crash onto each other, tongues entangle, gripping him by his neck, I pull him closer.

I need more.

He tastes like heaven—mint and ecstasy all rolled into one. I want nothing more than to live in this moment until the end of eternity—and even then, I don't think it would be enough. How on earth could I have denied my feelings for this man?

A loud scream from behind us has us breaking apart, breathless.

Holy shit. What just happened?

Laughing, he leans in and kisses me once more before saying, "What do you say we get out of here?"

Chapter 16
Jax

The moment we're in my truck, I'm dying to continue what we've started. Leaning across the console, I cup my hand along her cheek and press my lips to hers. The moment she opens her mouth to me, I let my tongue slip inside and mingle with hers. Heat explodes through my body and everything I've been holding back for weeks pours out. Sloane responds with a sense of urgency, making me forget the world around us exists.

That is until a car honks at the intersection, and I'm regretfully brought back to reality. We're not alone, and as much as I'd love to continue kissing her, we need to move this somewhere less public.

Sloane runs a finger over my lips as she grins. "As much as I could spend the rest of the day kissing you, we should probably leave."

Pulling out of the parking lot, I head back toward town. "I'm totally on board with that plan. Got anywhere in mind?"

Rolling her eyes, she grins conspiratorially. "I think I might know a place."

This woman is infuriating. "Are you going to tell me, or shall I just drive around in circles?"

"As much as I love spending time with you no matter what we're doing, I think I might combust if I don't get my mouth on yours soon."

Ohmigod, this woman.

Chuckling, I stop at a light and face her. "Well, we can't have that now. There's no need for combusting. I'll gladly volunteer to kiss you until you can't think straight, just for safe-keeping."

"I might just hold you to it, Jax. Good thing my place is close, and my sisters are at work."

"That's a very good thing indeed." I grin, eager for the light to change.

The moment we step through the door to her house, she grabs my hand and heads for the stairs. I'm led through a series of turns until we come to a door at the end of a hall.

The moment we enter the room, she turns and shuts the door, clicking the lock.

Reaching her arms round my neck, she grins. "Now that we're alone, what ever will you do with me?"

Words flow out of my mouth before I can stop myself. "I'd love to do everything imaginable to you." My body may be on board with anything she throws down, but I'm not a selfish asshole, and I won't take advantage of her either. "But for the record, I have zero expectations. I'm happy just spending time with you. You set the pace."

Sloane's smile is devilish as she fists my shirt in her hands. "The only expectation I have, Jax, is having your lips on mine."

Her request is granted before she finishes her last word. The electricity that's been zinging between us for weeks crackles. She meets me with the perfect combination of push and pull as she opens her mouth to meet mine. The grip on my shirt tightens, and she pulls me closer.

"God, you feel amazing," I mutter between kisses.

Snaking my arms around her waist, my fingers flirt at the hem of her shirt. I've never been more thankful for the ropes course. Sloane's sexy as hell in her black leggings and cropped green tee. It took everything in me to keep my hands off her when I picked her up.

As if they have a mind of their own, my fingers trace up her spine, making circles as I explore her soft skin. God, I've been dying to do this for days. When I realize there isn't much give in the material, I break our kiss and pant, "Take this off."

Sloane raises a brow in challenge. "Okay, but two can play this game, Rock Star." Reaching for the hem of my shirt, she says, "This has to go, too!"

Not wanting to waste time, I step back and pull it over my head in an instant. Just in time for me to see that sexy tongue of Sloane's swipe along her bottom lip, as she takes in every inch of my chest that's on display.

I've never been more thankful for working out than I am in this moment. My skin prickles as I feel her eyes roam in appreciation. As I step toward her, I remind her she's still fully dressed. Reaching for the hem of her shirt, I ask, "Can I help you with this?"

Nodding once, she says, "Sure."

The moment I pull her top free from her head, I take her in. She's in a black sports bra that displays her cleavage perfectly. Running a hand down my face to gather my thoughts, I step closer and moan, "God, you're beautiful."

I pull her close, so that we're chest to chest. "I wanna kiss every square inch of you," I promise as my lips meet hers.

Her hands feel magnificent as they trail along the muscles of my chest and around to my back. I'm instantly rock hard and can't wait to have my way with her. But for now, I'm determined to make this about Sloane.

My hands roam along her back to the perfect globes of her ass. God, she feels soft, yet firm in all the right places. This woman drives me wild. Needing more, I pull her close. Her body feels incredible against mine. Dying to explore the rest of her, I break our kiss, leaving her panting for air.

I love the way her body responds as I trail hot kisses along her jaw and down the column of her neck. From her sexy moans, I quickly find a spot that drives her wild. Breathlessly, she begs, "Oh, God, more, Jax. Right there."

Cupping her perfect breast in my hand, I give her what she wants. Sloane writhes and presses against my body as I find new ways to drive her wild. The most exquisite moan falls from her lips when I kiss along her collarbone to the swell of her breast.

She tastes fucking fantastic— a mixture of something sweet and spicy that I can't quite place, but forever in my mind will be engraved as Sloane. I could feast on her for days and never tire.

The fabric is tight and as my fingers skim under her bra, I'm forced to step back and ask, "Help?"

Grinning, she crosses her hands in front of her chest. Before I can take my next breath, her beautiful full breasts are freed from their confinement. I swear all the air I have rushes out as I take in her beauty. She's beautiful from the inside out, but I can't breathe, and I certainly can't speak because all the synapses to my brain are short circuiting.

This woman is a fucking goddess.

"See somethin' ya like?" she teases me when I'm frozen in place. Then when I don't respond, she cups her hands under her breasts and lifts them. "They're just boobs, Jax. See... they wiggle just like the rest of me."

"Oh my fucking God," I moan but make a point to only focus on her eyes. "For the record, before a single stitch of clothing was removed, I thought you were the most beautiful woman in the world. Now—" I swallow hard as my eyes roam her body. "You're hands down the sexiest woman I've ever seen, too."

Reaching for me, she whispers, "Show me."

And that's exactly what I do.

Our lips collide together, and our limbs intertwine. When I can't take any more, I lift her with ease, walking her to the bed, where I deposit her. She squirms toward the middle to make room for me, but I stop her. "Stay right there. Keep your legs at the end."

For a second, I can tell she's thinking about challenging me, so I quickly warn, "Sloane. Let me show you how beautiful you are. Let me taste every inch of you. Let me have my way with you. You're always in control, and right now—in this moment, you need to let go."

For the first time ever, her shoulders relax, and a sexy smile spreads across her gorgeous face. Then she whispers, "You always know just what I need."

"I'm determined to try," I promise as I lower my body over hers, kissing that grin off her face. I take my time, kissing down her body and across her breast. Gently squeezing one, to roll her nipple between my thumb and finger, my mouth latches onto the other, sucking hard.

"Oh, Jax," she moans, arching off the bed. "That feels incredible."

Taking my free hand, I slide my fingers down her thigh and back up to her core. Through the thin fabric of her pants, I can feel her heat and dampness. Cupping her mound, my fingers trace her folds through the fabric. Sloane squirms like crazy, and I know she wants more. Reaching for the waistband of her leggings, I ask, "Can I take these off?"

Nodding, she pants, "Yes."

Before I know it, she's slithering out of her pants and kicking them to the floor.

Sloane completely exposed is a sight to behold. Once again, my breath catches in my throat as I take in her body. She's soft, sexy, and absolutely stunning.

After a few heartbeats, my body unlocks from the hold she has on me. Leaning in to make good on my promise, I brush my thumb along her full lips. Meeting her eyes so there's no confusion, I tell her how I feel. "You are so beautiful, Sloane."

Starting over again, I kiss her from head to toe. She pants as she writhes against me as I explore each and every inch of her—except where she wants it most.

"Jax," she moans as I kiss up her inner thigh to her hip.

"Yes, Sloane," I prompt between kisses.

"Stop teasing me," she says, fisting my hair in her hand.

Running a finger from her slit to her clit, she's dripping with need.

"Tell me what you want," I say, dragging wet kisses along her lower abdomen.

It's sexy as hell when she takes what she wants and shoves my head lower. "This. Fucking make me come already. I'm not sure I can handle this torture much longer."

Laughing, I slide my tongue where my fingers had just been. Using my hands, I spread her wide and lick her sensitive flesh. She tastes fucking incredible. Licking from her center, I trail my tongue along her slit up to swirl around her clit. I repeat the motion and as she writhes under me, just when I don't think she can take any more, I plunge two fingers inside her and scissor them as I suck firmly on her sensitive clit.

Her hands fist my hair so tight, I swear I'll be bald when

this is over, but I don't fucking care. She fucking tastes incredible.

When a guttural growl erupts from her lungs, her legs tighten around my head like a vise. Immediately, her body pulses around my fingers for a split second before her entire body rocks with pleasure.

I refuse to change a single thing I'm doing until I'm certain I've coaxed every last ounce of pleasure from her. I won't be that guy who leaves her hanging midway through an epic orgasm. I want it all. I need to taste every last drop of her.

When her hands and legs relax and fall to the sides, I crawl up her body and look her in the eye. Her lids remain closed as she fights for her breath.

Brushing a strand of hair from her face, I whisper, "You okay?"

Without opening her eyes, she smiles. "I think you broke me in the most delicious way."

Leaning in, I kiss her once more. "Need me to put you back together again?"

"Maybe... can't move..." she draws out as her head flops to the side again.

God, she's fucking adorable blissed out. I hope I can keep her in this state as often as possible.

Chapter 17
Sloane

These last few weeks have been crazy to say the least. Between the festival starting tomorrow and every spare moment I spend with Jax, I'm living on adrenaline, caffeine, and great sex. My only saving grace is that ever since the ropes course, Jax has stayed at my place a few nights a week. I swear it's the only way we'd see one another.

Tonight, when he gets off work from the restaurant, we're hanging with my sisters at the beach for a bonfire. I'm so grateful they like him, or things would've been over before it started. It's my last night off before the festival is in full swing, so I want to make every moment count.

I'm finishing some last-minute things for work when I hear a knock at our door. Knowing it's likely Jax, I close my laptop and rush to answer. I'm surprised to find a stranger instead. "Raven?" he asks, clearly thinking I should know him. Before I can say anything, he mutters, "It's me... Loren... Uh... Well... this is weird." He looks at his watch. "Didn't you ask me to come by at seven?"

"I'm sure Raven did, but this is Sloane, her sister," Jax says, climbing the stairs behind him.

"Hey, babe, how was your day?" Jax asks, leaning in to give me a quick kiss.

Then he turns to Loren. "Hey, man, I thought that was you. How are you?"

Loren's face lights up with recognition. "Great to see you. I'm here to see Raven. Is she here?"

"She's already down at the beach with Lizzy. You're welcome to walk through the house to get there."

After letting him in, I lock the door. Then I point Loren in the direction of the deck, and we walk through the house together. "How long you in town for?" Loren asks Jax. Obviously, they must've grown up together.

"I'm just here for the summer. What are you up to these days?" Jax says as he opens the sliding door for us. Then he turns to me. "Got everything you need?"

Nodding once, I grab the bag I'd placed by the back porch.

As we walk down the steps, Loren continues their conversation, "I've just finished my sophomore year at CRU, then I'll go wherever I can get a job."

"I get that," Jax mutters, then he does something that melts my heart. "How long have you known Raven?"

"I've run into her a few times with friends. She invited me to come hang out tonight."

"Hmmm..." Jax says as he scrutinizes Loren. It's adorable how protective Jax is of Raven. But he should know she can hold her own.

We don't get the chance to say anything else. Once we crest the hill, Raven waves to us, and Loren is long gone. Reaching for Jax's hand, I pull him to a stop and whisper, "Don't get too attached to anyone Raven brings home. They usually don't stick around longer than a night or two."

"Loren was a year behind me in school, but he's a decent guy," Jax assures me.

"They're all decent guys, Jax. Raven doesn't date assholes. But she also doesn't let them stick around either. You know that, right?"

Scratching his head, he looks to my sister. "Uh, I've only seen her date that Bret guy."

"She's not looking for anything serious. So, if this guy turns into a stage nine cling-on, you'll have to help set him right, okay?"

Raising a brow, he asks, "You do this often?"

Shrugging, I admit, "Sometimes. Usually, she's upfront with a guy, and they don't have any issues with it. So, it doesn't happen often. I just don't want you to get your hopes up, since he seems to be a friend of yours."

Shaking his head, Jax laughs. "Sloane, I graduated with less than one hundred people. Of course, we're all friends. Or at least get along well enough."

Once we're all seated by the fire, Lizzy asks, "Are you ready for tomorrow night?"

Jax takes in a long breath and exhales slowly. "I'm as ready as I'll ever be. I've gotta say, if it weren't for your brilliant sister here, I likely wouldn't even be in this contest."

Puffing out my chest, I admit, "Hey, I know great talent when I see it. I've actually found three of the top thirty acts, thank you very much."

"Wow, that's incredible," Raven cuts in. "I'm so proud of you, Sloane."

Jax pulls me into his side, squeezing me tight. "So am I."

"Thanks," I say, hugging him back, not knowing what to say beyond that.

Jax and I talk about anything and everything under the sun, but we don't talk about the competition. I know he's nervous, but I truly think he has a shot. He's been selected to play later in the evening tomorrow because based on the promo I've given him, the execs at the record company think he'll draw a bigger crowd. Of course, he isn't privy to this information, as I don't want to add any unnecessary pressure.

By the time Lanie and Ryan join us for the bonfire, we have music playing on a portable speaker from Lizzy's phone. The fire is ready to cook hot dogs, and we're digging into the individual bags of chips and soda I brought for us to enjoy.

Once everyone has eaten, Lanie excitedly shouts over the music, "Hey, everyone, we've got another announcement to make! Can you turn the music down for a sec, Liz?"

After everyone settles, she gushes, "Ryan and I have the best news. Go ahead, Ry. Tell them."

Ryan grins from ear to ear and suddenly, I'm fully invested. He looks happier than a kid on Christmas morning. "Well, it looks like we've set a date. After talking with your dad, he's requested leave for at least two weeks next summer."

Lanie must think he's taking too long because she suddenly shouts, "We're getting married July first!"

All at once, we share our excitement. "That's fantastic," Lizzy gushes. Raven and I both say, "Congratulations."

Lanie looks to each of us and says, "I know you'll be busy, but we'd really like you to be a part of it."

"We wouldn't miss it for the world," I insist, knowing I speak for the rest of us. Why she would think otherwise is beyond me.

"Who knows..." Ryan draws in a deep breath, then looks to Jax with a wink. "If this guy isn't too rich and famous, maybe he'll consider playing for us at our little wedding."

Shaking his head, Jax guffaws, "Now you're just being ridiculous. When I'm still around—which I very well should be —I'd be happy to play your song for you."

With the excitement over, I lean into Jax and watch the flames dance across the fire. We're sitting on a blanket I brought out, and there's no place I'd rather be than wrapped up in Jax's arms.

As my sisters continue discussing wedding plans, I look into Jax's eyes, tapping his leg for his attention. "I know things will be crazy tomorrow. But I want you to know, I think you've got this, and I'll be rooting for you."

Leaning in, he kisses me on the lips, and I feel it deep in my belly as I anticipate what's to come. "I couldn't have done this without you."

Chapter 18
Sloane

Today is game day. I've been working my ass off for the entire summer, and now it's time to see if all my careful planning pays off. All the execs from the label are here, as well as the special judges for the competition. I've checked and double checked to make sure their needs are met. I've run through the lineup with the competitors, and they all know when and where they need to be. I've spoken with publicists, managers, parents of minors, and everyone involved, so fingers crossed, everything goes to plan.

The competition is much like many of those you see on TV. Each act was to prepare up to three songs to sing in front of the judges, though they'll only sing one officially. Their songs have a set time limit and have been approved by the producers to assure nothing goes awry.

I haven't seen Jax since the bonfire, as he went home to get a good night's sleep. I've been here since six this morning, and I'm part of the all-hands-on-deck team we have staying throughout the day.

Since I live in Seaside full time, and I'm the acting regional talent coordinator, I've had more responsibility than the temporary help the label's brought in to support this event. Tara and the rest of our team have been here all week, ensuring everything goes according to plan.

The first act is due on stage in twenty minutes. Most have checked in but are doing their own thing to stay focused on their performances. Even for midday, the beach is crowded, and the venue itself is fairly full. I can't imagine what it will be like later tonight. The venue is booked with big-named acts throughout the week, but tonight and Saturday night is designated for the competition. We're going from thirty acts to five tonight. The pressure is on, and the excitement buzzing around me is palpable.

As I walk through the crowd, I spot Trent Waters, the lead singer for the band Edgewater when he says, "Hey, Sloane, you're just the girl I'm looking for."

"What's up, Trent?" I ask, looking for the rest of his band.

Trent's the front man for an up-and-coming pop band. He's twenty-seven, with beautiful blue eyes and a full sleeve tattoo that makes girls go crazy. He's quite the performer, and the camera loves him. I love working with his band; they're fun, easygoing, and full of charm. They make my job easy, which I truly appreciate.

"Do you know a place where I can get a phone charger? Mine isn't working, and I need to stay in contact with the band. I can't let my phone die—today of all days."

"Yeah, that would suck," I agree. Looking around, I point to a tent set up for contestants. "There's a charging station in there, along with some snacks. I know we have quite a few in there."

"Thanks. But I'll be in town all week, so I'll need a new cord regardless. Can you point me in the direction of where I can pick one up?"

"I'd check The Phone Store off the main highway going toward Astoria. I know the grocery store will have some, but they'll charge you an arm and a leg for it."

"Thanks." He nods in appreciation.

"No problem," I assure him. "It's the benefit of being a local."

Spotting Tara from the corner of my eye, I start walking in her direction to check in with her, but Trent stops me. "Hey, before I forget, and things get crazy today... I wanna thank you for all the help and support you've given the band. Edgewater wouldn't even be here today if you hadn't pushed us." Reaching out, he pulls me into a bear hug.

He squeezes me so tight, I can't help but laugh. The man is a hugger. He has been since the night I found him in Portland. "Just doing my job, Trent."

With a chuckle, he sets me down. "Thank you so much for everything, babe. I owe you big time."

With that, he pats me on the shoulder and leaves for the tent.

I can't help but shake my head at what a whirlwind that man is. His entire band is brilliant, but part of their charm is you never know what you're going to get with them. I hope they do well in this competition.

Wanting to check in with Tara, I turn and look for her, but she's disappeared. Shoot. I'm sure if she needs anything, she'd text or call. Pulling out my phone to check my never-ending to-do list, I suddenly feel the nape of my neck tingle. When I look up, I'm met with Jax's beautiful smile.

"Hey, you." He leans in to brush a kiss to my cheek and pulls me in for a hug. God, he smells delicious and is just what I need after working all day. "I've missed you. How's it going so far?"

"It's..." Crazy, chaotic, exhilarating...all of which describe my day, but I stick with, "Going…" so he doesn't take on my stress as well as his own. Then I quickly add on to assure him, "Overall, everything's going according to plan. It should be a fantastic event."

Rocking back on his heels, he nods as he shoves his hands into his pockets and looks me over with care. "You're taking breaks, right?"

Gah, this man. Here he is, on possibly the biggest day of his life, worrying about me. "I'm good, Jax. It'll be a crazy week, and then I'll take a few days off and relax." If I weren't working in this moment, I'd have to kiss the living hell out of him for being so considerate.

Instead, I look him over to see how he's really doing. I know he's nervous, but in this moment, he appears as if he's got it together. As my eyes drag down his body, I know without a doubt, the girls will go crazy for him tonight. His black, well-fitted tee and well-worn jeans look sexy as hell, and I hope the judges love him as much as I do. Around his neck is a pair of headphones, and he's got a backpack over his shoulder.

"You ready?" I ask, feeling hopeful. I know he'll kill it tonight. He's just got to believe in himself.

Sucking in a deep breath, he exhales slowly. "As ready as I'll ever be. I know it's probably better to go toward the end, so I'll be fresh in the judges' memory, but I'd much rather just get this all over with."

"I'm sure this is stressful, but you've got this. Just get up on stage and show the world who Jax Cartwright is."

Rolling his eyes, he grumbles, "You make it sound so easy."

"Maybe find a way to relax and get your mind off things? You've got a few hours before you're set to go on stage. Just take a walk—but don't go too far. We need to be able to reach you should the schedule change."

"I know… I won't go far," he says on a laugh. "You don't

need to manage me. I refuse to be someone you need to worry about this week. You've got enough going on helping organize all this."

When my phone buzzes in my hand, I see that it's Tara. Pointing up my finger, I say, "I gotta take this."

"Hey, Tara, what's up?"

"I need you to track down Rick Turner. We need him on stage for the opening. I've tried texting him, but there's no answer."

"I'll look for him now."

The line goes dead, and I turn to Jax apologetically.

"I gotta run." Reaching out to take his hand, I squeeze it reassuringly. "If I don't see you again before your performance, please know I'm rooting for you. I can't wait to see you kill it on stage."

Pulling me in for a quick hug, he kisses my neck. God, he feels amazing. "You are the best medicine for my nerves."

I squeeze him tighter, wishing I didn't have to let go. "If only I could do more..."

"This helps, trust me," Jax whispers as he kisses my cheek again.

Letting go, I look him in the eyes to make my point clear. "I believe in you, Jax. I'm going to do what I can to check in on you in a bit. But I gotta run, or this show won't start on time."

Chapter 19
Jax

To pass the time, I put on headphones and find a quiet corner in the contestant area where I do my best to relax. My phone has been blowing up all day with people wishing me luck, and I just need to silence everything and unwind. My family is watching the show, and we're meeting soon in the VIP area to grab something to eat—though with the way my stomach feels, I doubt I'll eat much of anything.

I haven't spoken to Sloane, but I've seen her now and again as she checks in with various people throughout the day. Not that I'm a creeper but watching her float around the room, just knowing she's near, puts some of my nerves at ease.

Closing my eyes, I lean against the wall behind me, willing time to pass faster. I'd give just about anything to get this over with. I've listened to a few acts. Some were really good, and my nerves can't handle comparing myself to each and every one of them to see how I measure up. It's just not healthy for me in this moment.

No, I just need to go out there, get on that stage, and play the songs I've been working my ass off for these past few weeks.

I need to forget everything about this competition and just lay my heart on the line. If I don't leave it all on the stage, then what's the point of even doing this?

When a hand lands on my shoulder, my body jolts in a fight or flight response. My eyes spring open to find my dad smiling down at me apologetically. "I didn't mean to scare ya—but you didn't respond when I said your name."

Standing to my feet, I dust off my jeans. "Yeah, just tuning the world out... if ya know what I mean." Looking around I ask, "Where's Mom and Emily?"

"They wanted to give you some space. They'll be here in a minute but thought you may need our support in smaller doses to start out. It was your mom's idea. She caught a glimpse of you pacing earlier and thought we should check in."

Of course, she did. She always knows just what I need. "So did you draw the short straw?" I tease, trying to make light of the situation.

Chuckling, Dad shakes his head. "Naw. Selfishly, I had to see for myself that you're doing okay."

"Well... I'm hanging on by a thread," I admit. No sense in feeding my dad any line of BS. He'll know it just by looking at my face. He always has.

"Let's grab a table and get something to eat," he offers, pointing to the area where others are eating. "I'd bet my last paycheck you haven't eaten a bite today. I'd hate to have you get up on that big ole stage and pass out on us."

"Dad... I'm fine," I protest. "If I pass out, it certainly won't be from lack of food."

I follow Dad through the line while he grabs a roast beef sandwich from the tray and puts it on a plate. Then he adds a bunch of red grapes and a Cherry Coke from the cooler, all of which are my favorites. Then we make our way to a table that'll give us some privacy to talk.

When we sit down, he pushes his plate in front of me and demands, "Eat."

"I'm not really hungry," I admit as I lean back in my chair, crossing my arms over my chest.

"Well, I'm not either. But I'll tell you what. You take the first bite, eat what you can, and I'll finish the rest. I know you're not hungry, but you need food."

"Dad, you know I'm not six, right?" Why is he really doing this?

"Oh, don't I ever. When you were six, my biggest worry for you was whether or not you could make it all the way over to Jimmy Anderson's house on your bike." Chuckling, he adds, "Did I ever tell you that your mom made me follow you from a distance to make sure you got there safely?"

Well, that's a trip down memory lane I wasn't expecting.

"No... but what does this have to do with anything? Why are you bringing that up now?"

Shrugging, he opens the Coke. "Well, this is my way of checking on you. You and I both know you're nervous about tonight. Hell, I'd bet everyone in this room is, in some way or another. But it's *my* job to worry about you."

Sliding the can toward me, he asks, "What's your biggest fear in this moment?"

Okay. We're doing this—apparently. There's no more skating around the truth of why he's here.

Circling my finger around the rim of the can, I admit, "That I'll make an ass of myself."

He nods once, then asks, "How would you feel if you walked away right this moment?"

"I guess I would wonder if I was ever good enough to begin with."

"There's only one way of knowing. Do you believe you have a shot at moving to the next level?"

"Sloane seems to think I do," I counter, not really answering his question. "But if I make it to the final five, what will I do about the tour they've got planned?"

Dad cocks a brow as if I should know the answer to that, then deadpans, "You work on computers, right?"

Eyeing him suspiciously, wondering what the hell he's getting at, I snark in return, "Uh, you know the answer to that question."

"Last I checked, people were getting degrees online. Isn't that something you could do—and be on tour?"

"I suppose..." I ponder, wondering how I could make it work.

"Or you could always take a gap year. Isn't that what kids these days are doing? Take a year, see if this music thing pans out, then go back to college when you're done."

Chuckling, I can't believe my ears. "Who are you and what have you done with Charles Cartwright? Blink twice if you've been abducted by aliens and you're stuck in there, Dad."

This earns me a belly laugh.

When he finally catches his breath, he says, "Jax, you have the rest of your life to take the safe route. You're only young once. This might be the biggest risk you've ever taken, but it might also be your greatest reward. Big things don't happen unless we do the scary things."

Well, if that isn't a punch to the gut.

"Okay, point taken." Shaking my head, I reach for the sandwich in front of me. "I'm already doing one scary thing today. In fear of jinxing myself, I'd rather not make any other big decisions until I know they're actually an option."

"Nothing has to be decided today, Jax. But I never want you to look back and wonder."

As if on cue, my mom and sister choose that time to check

in. "Hey, sweetie, there you are," Mom says as she leans in for a hug. "How are you holding out?"

"I'm good," I admit honestly. "I plan to go out there and leave it all on the stage; the rest is out of my control."

"That's a great attitude." Emily grins, then pulls out her phone and leans toward me. "Let's take a selfie. You can post it on your socials. People are begging for proof of life. You've been radio silent all day."

"Uh, I've been a little busy," I say in defense.

Holding out her phone, she smirks. "Smile, or you'll look like an ass."

"Emily," Mom admonishes, though we all laugh.

She captures the perfect shot and says, "I'll just tag you. This is the perfect before shot."

"Before... As opposed to?" I ask, uncertain of what she's talking about.

"After you're famous." She leans in obnoxiously as if I should be following her train of thought to crazy town.

Laughing at her obnoxiousness, I shove her face away. "Shut up. You have no idea what you're talking about."

"Oh, big brother, I know exactly what I'm talking about. Mark my words."

Laughing, I must admit, my family knows how to get my mind off everything.

I'M STANDING OFF STAGE, waiting for the band ahead of me to finish, when I feel someone tap me on the shoulder. Turning, I'm surprised to find Sloane's beautiful face.

What a sight for sore eyes.

God, I've missed her.

Leaning in so that only I can hear, she whispers, "I don't

want to bug you as you get in the zone, but this is the first chance I've had to check in. You doing okay?"

Reaching for her hand, I squeeze it tight. "I'm better now that you're here."

"I can't wait for you to show the world who Jax Cartwright is. Your song choice is perfect, and I for one think you're gonna kill it."

The band before me hits their final note, and neither of us can speak over the noise. Sloane uses this time to lean in and kiss my cheek. I know she's working, but it means the world to me that she took this time to check on me.

The next thing I know, the emcee of the show says, "Ladies and gentlemen, our next act is a local musician, right here from Seaside, Oregon. Let's welcome to the stage, Jax Cartwright."

That's my cue to walk on stage. The lights are blinding, and I'm thankful to have them because it makes it so I truly can't see much of the audience. I'm not using a stool tonight, as it's only one song. I've chosen this song because it's a crowd favorite at Pop's as well as my most viral, according to Sloane.

As I walk on stage, my nerves linger, but I'm quickly put at ease by James Colins, the main judge for tonight's show. "Hi, Jax. I'm happy to have you here. Can you tell us all what you're singing for us tonight?"

Reaching for the mic, I step closer. "I'm singing a song I wrote, called 'Believing in Me.' At the time I wrote it, it wasn't about anyone in particular—but now I wish I'd written it about my biggest fan." Turning to Sloane, I say, "Thanks for believing in me."

"Are you ready?" another judge named Janet asks.

Nodding, I wait for the emcee to make my final introduction. "Let's make some noise for Jax Cartwright, everyone!"

Once I strum the first chord, time ceases to exist. My nerves are left behind as I transport to this place in my head where it's only me and my music. I pretend that instead of being on stage in front of thousands, I'm merely singing this to Sloane in her bedroom, as I've practiced a few times over the last week or so.

I sing about taking a chance on something and giving it my all. I sing about not knowing how to move on, until I found the person who believes in me. Leaving my heart and soul on the stage, I give this performance my all. As I sing my final note, I'm brought out of my trance by deafening screams and applause.

The lights are turned down, and I finally catch a glimpse of just how many people are here. Holy shit. I'm so glad I couldn't see anything before I went on. This crowd is insane. I never imagined playing for a group this big.

When the lights return and the emcee says, "Let's hear it again for Jax Cartwright." I remember to bow, smile, and wave like they told us to in the preshow meeting yesterday.

If I thought my adrenaline was pumping after a show at Pop's, it has nothing on how I feel in this moment. Words can't describe the energy zipping through my veins. I've never felt so alive.

As soon as I exit the stage, I walk straight into Sloane's awaiting arms. "You did it!"

Unable to control my excitement, I reach my hand behind her neck and pull her in for a sensual kiss. One that shows she's the reason I'm flying this high. She's the one who pushed me to get on that stage and sing my fucking heart out. I—fucking—did it! I conquered one of my biggest fears, and I know exactly what I want to do for the rest of my life.

When we break apart for air, I lean down, pressing my forehead to hers. I excitedly ask, "Now what?"

Chuckling, she kisses me chastely before shaking her head as her eyes dance in anticipation. "We wait."

Chapter 20
Sloane

Jax's pent-up energy flows through us as we fling ourselves through my bedroom door. We kiss in the stairwell, and I don't know how long it took us, but we just now made it to my room. Waiting to leave the competition was torture. I couldn't wait to celebrate with him properly.

Wanting to feel every inch of him, I drag his shirt up his muscled chest, kissing his sexy body as I go.

"I'm gonna kiss every square inch of you," I promise.

"You won't hear me complain." Jax chuckles, ripping his shirt over his head. "But if I'm getting naked, so are you."

Quickly removing my shirt and bra, I slide my hands to the buckle of his belt, Jax's eyes fill with liquid heat as a moan escapes his lips in anticipation. It takes no time at all to undo his belt and have his jeans crumpled on the floor.

Damn. This man is so sexy and with the way he's looking at me, I might become his next meal. But first, I'm determined to have my way with him.

Kissing the hard planes of his chest, I reach into his boxer briefs and stroke his lengthening cock. I can't wait to ride him later, but now, I'm dying for a taste.

"Oh... Sloane... You're driving me fucking crazy."

"In the best way possible, I hope," I tease, licking down his abs.

Needing a better angle, I drop to my knees, taking his boxers with me to the floor. His glorious cock springs free, begging for attention.

Knowing it drives him wild, I cup his balls as I gently squeeze his length. Desire flows through me as his cock somehow hardens further in my fist. Licking my tongue along my lips in anticipation, I lean forward and take him in.

Sweeping my tongue under the head of his cock, I swirl around the tip. When a low moan escapes, I take things up a notch by fisting his base and sucking him in deep. In and out, my tongue swirls around the tip before moving down and taking him in to the hilt.

"Fuck... Sloane... That feels good."

His hands fist my hair as he guides me just how he likes it.

I take this as my cue to hollow my cheeks and suck harder.

Up and down, my lips never leave his shaft as I flatten my tongue to create more friction.

Just when I think he's going to let me finish him this way, he stops me by pulling his cock free.

"What's wrong?" I ask, completely confused.

"Ohmigod, you feel amazing," he pants, "but I'm dying to taste you."

He must read the disappointment on my face because he suddenly demands, "Strip and get on the bed. I want your mouth on my cock and your pussy on my face."

My core clenches at the thought of it.

"I love it when you talk dirty like that. It makes me wet and needy."

For a second, he just stares at me, and I'm afraid I've gone too far. But my boldness must turn him on.

With a devilish grin, he slowly strokes his cock as he demands, "Well, get your sexy ass on that bed, so I can taste that exquisite pussy of yours. I want you on all fours with your ass in the air so I can lick your tight cunt and make you come while you go down on me."

"Holy shit, that was hot," I admit as I shed my clothes, then scramble onto the bed. I've never done anything like this before, but with Jax, I'm willing to try all sorts of new things.

"After I make you come with my tongue, I'm gonna fuck you all night."

"If you keep talking like that, I might come from your voice alone," I admit.

Leaning in to speak directly in my ear, he says, "Once I have you coming on my tongue, I'll use this mouth of mine any way you want it."

Within seconds, he's got me right where he wants me, and I'm feasting on his velvety-hard cock. Fisting the base with one hand, I pump his shaft while I slip my tongue around the tip. Then I take him in and suck hard, only to slide back up and start again. At times, I'm barely able to concentrate, but somehow, I manage.

He's gripping my hips with his hands, while his thumbs have me splayed apart to give him access. His tongue is wicked as he licks along my slit to circle my clit.

Oh. My. Fucking. God. I don't think I can take this much more.

As I feel my spine tingle, energy pulses through me. My legs shake, and I freeze, trying to concentrate on making this feeling last.

Jax somehow manages to slip a finger into my dripping core as he latches onto my clit and sucks hard. Within seconds, I'm tumbling over the edge. Pulse after pulse, my body quakes with absolute pleasure.

Jax doubles down on his efforts and before I know it, I'm begging him to stop because I can't take any more. My clit is beyond sensitive, and I need a moment to recover.

Letting me fall to the side, he quickly repositions his body so we're facing one another. "You okay, beautiful?"

Grinning, I admit, "I'm better than okay."

Then I lean in to kiss him. What starts out as a sweet kiss soon turns to sensual when I feel his pulsing cock brush against my leg. Reaching between us, I stroke it a few times. "We need to do something about that," I tease.

"I'm trying to give you some time to recover, babe. You created a fantasy I want to fulfill."

"Really?" I ask, feeling turned on. "What's that?"

A smile plays at his lips as he leans in to speak directly in my ear. "I want you at the end of the bed on all fours. I want to spank that beautiful ass of yours for making me talk dirty and get all these thoughts in my head. Then I want to go balls deep from behind until I come inside you."

Leaning in to kiss him once more, I say, "God, I love it when you talk like that. Let's make that fantasy of yours a reality."

Chapter 21

Jax

Oh my God, if I thought waiting to perform was torture, it's got nothing on waiting for the results. I've been on pins and needles for the past twenty-four hours. Tonight, the rest of the competitors performed. Then the winner from last year performed a few songs so the judges could deliberate.

Sloane got swept away to help with something, and I've been sitting here in the contestant area, trying to act like I'm not going out of my mind. On the outside, I'm certain I look as though I'm aloof and merely sitting in this chair, awaiting results. My only tell would be the tapping of my palm against my leg. But I've got headphones on, attempting to listen to music because I just can't be alone with my thoughts.

Even at this high volume, intrusive thoughts still seep in. I'm scrutinizing every moment of my performance, wondering if I hit it just right. Wondering if there was anything more I could've done. Each thought comes back with the same result— *no, I did everything I could*. It'll simply be up to the judges to determine whether or not I'm what they're looking for.

Eventually, one of the stage crew comes and taps me on the shoulder. "Jax?"

Taking off my headphones, I ask, "What's up, man?"

"You're wanted on stage with the rest of the contestants. They made an announcement, but I don't think you heard it."

Standing to my feet, I shove my headphones in my backpack and shake off my nerves. Following him to where they need me, I focus on my inner monologue.

I repeatedly tell myself, I'm okay with whatever is about to happen. I may not make it to the next round, but this experience proves that music is important. It's something I'll continue no matter what happens in the next few minutes.

God, until this moment, I never knew how much I really wanted this. But maybe that's a good thing. I didn't have to stress over it either.

Chuckling at how absurd it was to take this so lightly, I step out onto the stage for perhaps my final time. I stand where a stagehand directs me, and I wait for others to be placed around me. The lights are off to keep the suspense, but I'm grateful because it means I can keep my thoughts to myself a while longer.

My nerves are so out of whack when the emcee starts by thanking everyone for being here once again. They mention something about our sponsors and what's at stake for those who move on in the competition.

I tune it out because I just can't process this information.

I can't seem to make myself look at the other contestants or at the crowd in front of me. I choose to stare at a scuff mark at the front of the stage, so it doesn't look like I'm stupidly staring at my feet. My stomach rolls, and my nerves take flight like a flock of seagulls finding a fry on the beach, as the emcee continues his explanation. I'm sure it's good for the sake of the show, but the more he drones on, the more I just want to scream, "Tell us already."

Finally, the lights dim, and the anticipation music begins.

My fucking nerves are a wreck. I'm not sure I can take any more of this.

"Now, for the first of the final five contestants moving on from tonight's performance are..." He pauses for dramatic effects. "Monica Simms..." The crowd erupts, and a petite blonde a few people away from me bursts into tears.

I'm right there with you, sister. The anticipation is excruciating.

Once the crowd settles, the emcee continues, "The Fast Lane."

This time, an alternative rock band jumps up and down with excitement. I didn't listen to them perform, but from the way everyone cheers, they must've been good.

Of course, my logical side chooses this time to remind me that with each act selected, the chances of me making it get smaller.

I seriously didn't know how much I wanted this... until tonight. I'd originally participated to prove to myself I could just get on stage and perform... but never had serious thoughts I would make it that far. These people around me are all tremendous talents. It's an honor to be in this competition with them. But now that I'm on stage, awaiting results, I'll admit I want it more than I realized.

"Edgewater..."

This is one of the acts Sloane found and brought to the competition. The one the lead singer was hugging her when I found her this morning. I'm happy for them. They were really good.

Once the crowd has settled, the emcee announces, "Craving Spoons..."

An all-girl punk band from the other side of the stage bursts into screams, and they jump up and down with joy. It takes a while for everyone to calm down, and I wait on pins and needles to be put out of my misery.

Waiting—sucks—period. I can barely breathe when the crowd settles.

Finally, the announcer continues, "And last... but certainly not least... from right here in Seaside... our final contestant moving forward is none other than... Jax Cartwright."

I don't even process the words until the woman beside me reaches out and pulls me into a hug, screaming, "Congratulations!"

Holy shit... I made it....

Letting out a "Whoop," I return the hug, then set her down, shaking hands and hugging those who congratulate me as they walk off stage.

We were told the ones moving forward in the competition are to remain on stage while the others exit. Shifting so that we're closer to one another, the five remaining acts each congratulate one another for making it this far. I know it's still a competition, but I genuinely am grateful to be here with them.

When I get to Trent, the lead singer of Edgewater, he grips my hand like a vise and pulls me in for a hug. "Our girl did it! She got us to the next level. Hot damn, we're going on tour!"

"Holy shit... we are!" I say in disbelief. This is so fucking unbelievable! I still haven't processed the ramifications of being selected.

Everything that happens after the announcement is a complete blur. We're pushed through photographs, talking with VIP ticket holders, and congratulated by the judges.

My family is so excited, even my dad jumps up and down with excitement when they greet me. Unfortunately, I'm pulled away by one of execs from the record label, so we don't get to celebrate long. Randy works specifically with my genre and tells me he can't wait to hear more of what I've got. I do my best to concentrate, but I probably only comprehend half of our conversation.

By the time I find Sloane, she's taking pictures with the members of Edgewater. Trent and their drummer have their arms around her, as the rest of the band files in around them. A cameraman is going crazy taking photos as the group hoots and hollers with excitement. Sloane's never looked more beautiful.

The moment Sloane's eyes meet mine, her eyes light up, and she quickly excuses herself.

"I was wondering when I'd catch up with you," she says as I pull her into my arms for the embrace I've been desperately craving since this chaos began. "I'm so freaking happy for you." She smiles.

"Thank you for pushing me... for believing in me," I whisper into her ear as I squeeze her tighter. When I set her down, I exclaim, "Can you believe it? I fucking made it to the top five! I'm going on tour!"

Sloane's hazel eyes sparkle as she reaches for my hand. "I knew you had what it takes. You just had to believe it for yourself."

Sloane's boss, Tara, interrupts us, as she gushes from across the room, "There you are, Sloane! I've been looking for you everywhere!"

Laughing, Sloane looks around and points out, "I've been right here. What's going on? Do you need something?"

"I've come to tell you the news myself!" Tara practically shouts in excitement.

Sloane clearly has no idea what Tara's so excited about, so she asks, "What news?"

"We were going to wait until the end of the festival to

announce this because we wanted to be sure. But after talking with the other execs at the label, we all agree it should be now."

When Tara pauses for dramatic effect, Sloane clarifies, "What are you talking about?"

Reaching out her hand, Tara pats Sloane's arm. "Sloane, given the fact you've managed to wrangle not one, but two incredibly talented acts into this competition—who were nobodies before the festival, *I might add*—into the top five contestants. We want to officially make you the regional talent coordinator at Smashing Waves Records. You'll no longer be an intern, just filling in. You're getting a seat at the table in the exec board room."

Covering her mouth in shock, Sloane shouts, "Ohmigod, are you serious?"

Nodding profusely, Tara adds, "Yep. You're getting a promotion—that includes a huge raise compared to intern wages. This will also mean you'll be joining these acts on tour to scout for local talent while they're between performances."

Looking to me, Sloane gushes in disbelief. "Can you believe it? This is fantastic!"

Looking around at us guys, Tara fans herself. Then she looks back to Sloane. "Sloane, you've done a great job helping organize this event. I'm not sure what you're doing to find all these swoon-worthy acts." She looks to the guys around the room, then adds, "But keep doing it. Keep using your power of persuasion to get us more extremely talented, yet unknown acts like this to sign with the label. I know you'll do whatever it takes to make them shine—just like you have with these guys! They are living proof of your success!"

"Oh my gosh. This is incredible. But they're the real talent. Without them, I'd have nothing to promote."

Tara looks to her pointedly. "Honey, don't sell yourself short. You found both of these acts on your own. Neither of them had ever thought of performing at this level, and you worked your magic to make it happen. You knew what was riding on this summer internship, and you worked your ass off. You deserve this. I see great things ahead for you at Smashing Records, Sloane. Congratulations!"

As much as I'm excited for Sloane, there's something about the way Tara said that last part that rubs me the wrong way. My stomach rolls, as I consider her words once again.

Sloane knew a huge promotion was riding on this.

She knew if we performed well, she'd have a better chance of getting it.

I never would have taken a chance at this competition if she hadn't persuaded me.

Then there's that comment Trent made earlier. "*Our girl did it! She got us to the next level. Hot damn, we're going on tour!*"

Holy. Fucking. Shit.

What kind of persuasion did she use with the guys in Edgewater?

Tara said it herself. Sloane was persuasive, and none of us would apparently be here without her.

Is Sloane just *my* girl?

As I look around the group, I see Trent step closer to her and place an arm over her shoulder.

"Congratulations, babe. We couldn't be prouder of you."

Holy. Fucking. Shit.

Sloane used me.

Chapter 22
Sloane

After Tara made the announcement, I was pulled away from the group to talk with Jason, the guy I'll be working with to coordinate finding talent while on tour. We didn't talk long, just set up a time to meet later this week before he heads back to LA.

When I return, Jax is nowhere to be found.

Pulling out my phone, I shoot off a text.

Me: Where are you?

Jax: At home. Too tired to talk.

Well, I'm sure he's wiped out. Today was nerve wracking for everyone. But I was hoping he'd still be amped up after that killer performance and want to celebrate both our success tonight.

Sighing, I start to type....

Me: Come celebrate with me.

But I think better of it and go with this instead.

Me: Okay. Get some rest.

Something feels off with Jax, but I can't imagine what it would be. I've seen him survive off literally two hours of sleep all day if it meant spending just a little time together. He's always so pumped up after playing, he usually can't sleep for hours. His sudden disappearance doesn't make sense.

Today, I've been at work since nine. I'm helping with some of the signed artists the label has performing this afternoon. With the festival in full swing, there's no rest in sight for me.

Of course I brought my laptop, so I can make some promo for the finale. I know many others can do it, but I want to hype up Jax and Edgewater, since I've been doing it from the beginning. Their fans will be so proud of both of their performances.

Once the festival is over, Tara wants to talk specifics about my new job. One thing I need to disclose is my relationship with Jax. There was nothing against it as an intern, but I want to keep her privy with it going forward.

With only a few weeks until the tour officially begins, there's so much to do. I'm not sure how I'll feel riding on a bus around the country. I've never wanted that for myself, but if it means I get to spend more time with Jax, I'll consider it a win. Tara did say something about hotels, but we'll work out those details later, I'm sure.

With another show about to start, I realize I haven't heard from Jax all day. That's unusual. Even when he's worked a double at the restaurant, he'd always find time to at least text me and check in.

Maybe he thinks I'm too busy?

Needing to hear from him, I pull out my phone and send a quick text.

Me: Thinking of you.

The message goes from received to read. The dots start moving around, indicating he's responding, but disappear. I wait a few minutes, trying to busy myself with work, but my mind keeps going to Jax.

This is so unlike him.

He always texts back.

An hour goes by and still no answer. What the hell is going on?

I would call, but with the noise, I'd never hear him. It's driving me nuts. Something is clearly wrong. Jax has never gone radio silent for an entire day. If I weren't committed to being here all night, I'd drive my ass over to his house and demand answers.

By the time I get home, it's late. My nerves are on edge. Jax has gone an entire day without responding. I've already changed into my pajamas, and I'm sitting on the couch, staring at my phone for God only knows how long when Raven walks in from her night out with friends.

One look and she's crossing the room.

"Uh-oh. What's going on and who do I need to take care of?"

"Jax."

Just that one word has my well-constructed walls crumbling in an instant.

"What's going on? The two of you should be on cloud nine. Everything you've been working for is finally happening."

"I know," I say through watery eyes. "I don't know what changed. But he just disappeared last night and hasn't responded to me all day. Something is off."

"Sloaney," Raven coos as she snuggles in with me on the

couch. "He's probably just busy. I mean his life just changed at the drop of a dime. Give him some time to adjust."

Shaking my head, I insist, "No. Something's up. One minute, we're all celebrating and the next, he vanished into thin air."

Pulling out my phone, I shove it in her face.

"Look..." I point to the first message. "Look at these texts. I sent the first one within twenty minutes of receiving the news from Tara. He's always jacked up so high after he performs, there's no way he was too tired to talk. Usually, he's wired for hours. I'm just not buying this."

"It was a huge day for him, Sloane. He might've just been exhausted. I can't imagine what he went through to wait around all day, and then find out his life changed in an instant. I would've crashed for days after the adrenaline rush."

"But that doesn't excuse the fact he's been radio silent today. Now, it's well after midnight..." I draw out, willing myself not to cry. "It's too late to reach out and since he lives with his parents, I can't just show up there and demand to know what the hell is going on."

I. Will. Not. Cry.

Dammit. I will not cry.

"Oh, sweetie," Raven says as she brushes hair from my face. "You're tired, emotional, and have had an overwhelming week —and it's not even over. You need rest. Your nerves are fried because you're burning the candle at both ends. Get some sleep and see if he responds tomorrow."

"That's just it. I have a meeting with Tara at eight, and I'll be working the event until the winner is announced. I don't have time to get to the bottom of this. But something is wrong, Raven. I can feel it. He literally just walked away and has been avoiding me ever since."

"I'll tell you what. You go upstairs and sleep. If he hasn't responded by the morning, I'll track down that rat-bastard and give him a shake down."

Ohmigod. I can totally picture her doing just that.

"Really? You'd do that for me? Though he may not be worthy of being called a rat-bastard," I admit, not wanting to release Raven's wrath upon Jax unnecessarily. I remember the time she beat the crap out of Devin Jordan when we were eight —all because he called me a string bean and kept pulling my pigtails on the playground.

"I just know something is off, and I don't have time to get to the bottom of it. Tomorrow is a big day for him and no matter what's going on between us, he has to be at the top of his game. He's got too much riding on this to not be at his best."

"Oh, Sloane, you love him."

It's not a question or an accusation, just a fact, that only Raven would get so quickly.

Dammit. She's right.

I wasn't supposed to fall in love.

Nodding, I finally break, and tears flow down my cheek.

"I do, Raven. I'm not sure how he wormed his way into my heart so quickly..."

Wiping at my eyes, I suck in a deep breath so I can finish my thought clearly. "But his happiness matters to me; I just want to make sure nothing is wrong.

"If I don't hear from him by the time I go to work tomorrow, could you at least check in and make sure he's okay? I just can't get over his sudden disappearance. *Something* had to trigger it, and I can't for the life of me fathom what it is."

"Look," Raven says, demanding my attention, "you need sleep. Or you'll be the haggard twin with all the wrinkles when we get older."

"What. The. Hell?" comes out on a laugh. "Why are you so mean?"

"Got you to laugh, didn't I?" Raven smirks, and I shove her face away from me.

"But seriously, I'll shoot you a text when I wake up. Hopefully, Jax just needed to unplug for the day. But if you haven't heard from him, I'll track him down and take care of things."

I pull my sister in for a hug. "I love you forever." I don't know what I'd do without Raven in my life. She always knows just what I need.

Holding me for longer than necessary, Raven whispers, "I love you always."

Chapter 23

Jax

I have been a miserable son of a bitch since I walked away from Sloane. I haven't slept. I can't eat. I'm supposed to get up in front of thousands of people and sing tonight, and I could seriously care less.

As my dad would say, my give-a-fuck is broken, and I don't know how to fix it. I can't count how many times I've gone through every encounter I've had with Sloane. She's always been focused on work and extremely driven—that's never changed.

I knew from the start that I wanted more with Sloane. Hell, I'm the one who made those ridiculous ultimatums to keep finding ways to see her again. Was I just stupid and fell prey in her trap?

There's a knock on my door, and knowing my parents have already left for work, I grumble to Emily, "Go away. I'm still not ready to talk." She's been trying to talk since the contest.

To my surprise, the door opens, and my breath catches in my throat. God, is she a sight for sore eyes. But I still can't let her come in and get her way.

Jumping up from my bed, I rub the sleep from my eyes, hoping this isn't a mirage. "Wh... What are you doing here?"

Punching her hands to her waist, she quirks a brow. "I should ask you the same thing, dumbass! Your sister let me in to knock some sense into you."

Oh, shit. This is most definitely not Sloane. They may look alike, but that's about where their twin similarities stop. As I take her in, she's wearing ripped jeans, a cropped hoodie, and her hair is in a messy bun. This is nothing Sloane would wear when she's due at work at any moment. "What are you doing here, Raven?"

"Oh, so you can tell us apart. Yay you," she snarks. "Why the hell are you acting like a petulant child and ghosting my sister? You know as well as I do that this is literally the busiest week she'll have all summer. She doesn't have time for this shit, and frankly, neither do I."

"Why do you even care? Or did Sloane not let you in on her act?"

For a moment, Raven's jaw drops. "Act? What the hell are you talking about?"

"Oh, your sister can be very persuasive. I wonder how many others she's used?"

"Jax. You are this close to crossing a line that I'm not sure you'll recover from. Back up and start from the beginning."

There's something in her tone that makes me hesitate, and some of the steam I've been holding onto releases.

"Why exactly are you here, Raven? Why isn't Sloane here herself?" I demand.

"For starters, she's working. You know—that little competition you're supposed to perform in later this afternoon? Well, my sister's working her ass off and still has the time to worry about you."

"But why are *you* here specifically? Does she need you to come and check on her little project?"

Raven blows the hair from her face, frustration evident as she fists her hands at her sides. "Jax, I am here to check on you because my sister is worried. She knows something is wrong, but since you won't pick up the freaking phone and talk to her like an adult, she asked me to see for myself if you're okay."

"Well, as you can clearly see, I'm not. I haven't talked to Sloane because it hurts too fucking much to even think about her. I fell for her act hook, line, and sinker. She's all I can think about. When Tara told her to keep using all her persuasive tactics to get more acts, I just couldn't take it anymore. I had to leave. She used me, just like she used the guys in Edgewater. Trent was so proud that *our girl* got us to the next level in this competition any way she could. What a fool I'd been to think I was the only one for her."

Crossing her arms over her chest, she narrows her eyes.

"Jax, you're not making any sense. Sloane didn't use you—or the guys from Edgewater. I'm not sure why Trent would taunt you like that but trust me—my sister only has eyes for your dumb ass." Shaking her head, she mumbles, "Though I'm beginning to wonder why."

"Are you sure about that?" I counter. "You really think I'm the only guy Sloane's interested in?"

"Dude, I've never seen her more in love with anyone in my life. I do have to question her judgement though if you're gonna act like a complete prick now that you're getting the success she's helped you achieve."

I take a moment to process her words. "Wait... are you saying there isn't anyone else for Sloane?"

"Jax—" She hesitates as if she's choosing her words carefully. "You've got to be the dumbest man on this planet if you think my sister is involved with anyone else. She doesn't date musicians, but for some reason, she took a chance on you—please don't prove her theory about them right."

Replaying the scene from the contest in my mind, I realize I might have gotten it wrong. "I'm so confused," I admit, running my fists through my hair.

"So am I. Why don't you finally back up and tell me what happened?"

Each of us sits on the edge of my bed, and slowly, I go step by step through each thing that happened from the moment my name was called as part of the top five. I explain Trent's comments, which rubbed me the wrong way, as well as what Tara had said. By the time I'm done, I see that many of the statements could've been interpreted in multiple ways.

"Oh my God, I've been such a fool," I admit when I finally see the night for what it was.

Chuckling, Raven agrees. "Yeah. You are. But honestly, I think emotions were running high for you. You might've let jealousy seep in, and I'll be honest, between Trent and Tara's comments, I can see where you could make that leap. Especially when Sloane essentially confirmed it without knowing what you were really talking about."

"Do you think she'll give me another chance?" I ask desperately.

"Jax, Sloane has no idea the rabbit hole your brain went down. Hell, I can barely understand it myself entirely. I'll make you a deal. I won't let her know what an idiot you've been, if you promise not to put her through this shit again. If you can't communicate with her, you don't deserve her."

"You're right," I admit. "I don't."

"No more pity parties. If you're in with Sloane, you need to be all in."

"Is it okay to love you a little for setting me straight? But for the record, I'm completely *in love* with your sister." I chuckle.

Bumping her shoulder against mine, she laughs. "I can be on board with that. But I do have one more question. What's your plan to make things right with Sloane?"

A smile forms on my lips as a brilliant idea hits me. "Just make sure she's watching tonight."

Chapter 24
Sloane

No kidding. The show starts in less than an hour. What the hell has she been doing all day? Before I can ask, another message comes through.

Hmmm... That's fast. She must already be on her way. I use this time to check in one last time with all the acts.

Everyone is here, except Jax, and I'll admit, I'm still freaking out a bit.

I trust my sister and if she says everything is fine, it will be. But it doesn't mean my nerves haven't been wrecked for the last two days. When this festival ends, I need to crawl in bed and sleep for a week.

When Raven arrives, she's quite helpful. Not only does she put my mind at ease simply because she's here, but she also helps with little tasks that allows me to focus on other things. I've never been more thankful for her than I am in this moment.

Unlike the first part of this competition, I'm able to sit and watch the final acts perform in the VIP section near the stage— as there wasn't any last-minute things I needed to personally attend to. At least that's what both Tara and Raven insist on.

Raven assures me things are fine with Jax, but I have yet to see him for myself, so my stomach is in knots not only over his performance tonight—but for whatever the fuck is going on between us.

Or not going on between us at this point. Let's face it, if he won't even talk with me, there can't be an us in the future.

How the hell will we go on tour and work together if we can't even communicate with one another? My stomach clenches at the thought. I can't let myself go there.

Raven reaches over and clutches my hand in hers, giving it a squeeze. It's as if she knows the vicious thoughts swirling around in my brain and knows I need her support. For once, she's not the person I need most—and I'll admit that thought alone scares me more.

How has Jax become so important in such a short period of time?

Raven leans in and says, "You're overthinking. Stop."

"Like that's even possible," I snark. "You know me best of all. I'm an overthinker; it's what I do."

"Sloaney, you've got nothing to worry about. Trust me. Everything will work out. Jax can't talk to you because he's doing his pre-show things with the producers. Apparently, there was a change in the lineup, so he's working out the details."

"What?" I exclaim. "Why do you know that and I don't?"

Shrugging, she says, "He mentioned something in passing when I saw him backstage. He was in a hurry, so I didn't get any other details than that."

"But..." I go through all the possibilities of disaster he could encounter, however Raven cuts me off.

"You know deep down that he'd tell you himself if he could. Just relax and watch the show."

So far, we've watched The Fast Lane and Monica Simms perform. Each were pretty good, though I couldn't really enjoy their performance because I'm too preoccupied. Jax was supposed to go next, but apparently, the producers want Craving Spoons to switch places with him.

From firsthand experience, I know a lot goes on behind the scenes when decisions are made. I can't help but wonder if they're putting Edgewater and Jax at the end because they have a shot at winning it all? Or perhaps something else happened that I'm not privy to. Either way, I'm on edge.

Edgewater blows me away with their song "Misbehave." They brought it all and left everything they've got on stage. I'm so proud of Trent and the guys. They've come so far from playing at a local pub in Portland to this. They deserve to be on a big stage lighting the world on fire with their work.

Somehow, watching Edgewater kill it tonight calms my nerves, and I'm eager to see Jax perform. Not only will I get to see for myself that he's okay, but he'll finally get to perform the song "*Savage*" that he's been holding back to keep as his secret weapon for the competition. It's hands down the best song in his arsenal. I can't wait for the world to see it.

When it's time for Jax to take the stage, I see a member of the stage crew place a stool—which wasn't a part of the plan. What the hell is Jax doing?

The stage is dark, but Jax strides with confidence across the stage to sit on the stool. He takes a moment to adjust the mic, and my eyes never leave him as I watch him wait for his official introduction.

"For the final act in tonight's competition, we have a talented local from right here in Seaside joining us. Please give a hand and join us in welcoming...Jax Cartwright..."

The lights go on, and my heart stalls as I finally see Jax illuminated on the stage. As if he knows exactly where to find me, his eyes meet mine, and he nods once in my direction. I can tell he's nervous, but I hope like hell he can shake off whatever's been bothering him and give it his all.

"Now... let's see here," James Collins, the judge, starts, then looks to his notes. "You were originally planning to play the song that's been going viral, 'Savage,' but I've been told you have something else for us instead."

What? This isn't the plan. Why is he doing this?

"Thanks for letting me change things up a bit at the last minute. I hope you enjoy my new song I wrote today, 'Just Being Me.'"

What the hell is going on? Contestants can't just change their songs mid-show.

Looking to Raven, I ask, "Is this what he was talking with the producers about? 'Savage' is a hit, so why would he risk that?"

Shrugging, Raven whispers, "I have no idea."

"Well, this is certainly risky. But we wish you the best of

luck," James says, and I couldn't agree more. This makes zero sense.

"With no further ado... Here's Jax Cartwright performing his freshly written song, 'Just Being Me.'"

The song starts out with a catchy upbeat tempo and after a few chords, the crowd screams in appreciation—at least he's off to a good start. My spine trembles in anticipation as I await the lyrics.

You're the sweetest girl, who rocked my world
You came from out of the blue
And I never knew I could be free
Just being me

This is actually pretty good. Did he really write this today? I'm impressed. As I look around the venue, I can tell I'm not the only one enjoying this. When I look back to Jax, his eyes lock on mine, and he continues the second verse.

You were the sign that it's time to unwind
You let the weight of the world disappear
As you took a chance on me
Just being me

The instrumental break between verses revs the energy in the room. I can't wait for more. How could he have written this today?

You made me see that I found my voice
I don't need to stay safe because I've made the
choice
To believe in me
Sloane, you set me free

Holy shit. This song is about me.

Tears prick at the corners of my eyes as the words sink in. He fucking wrote a song about me—today. How is this possible?

> ***You're one of a kind, who speaks her mind***
> ***You took my world by surprise, making me***
> ***realize***
> ***You set me free***
> ***I love you for seeing me***

"Wait… Did he just say he loved me?"

"He told you and everyone else here that he loves you," Raven chimes in with a hip bump. "Shut up so I can listen to the rest of the song. It's really good."

> ***I hope you don't ask how fast did I fall***
> ***With you by my side, we can get through it all***
> ***You are it for me***
> ***I can clearly see***
> ***I'm in love with you***
> ***Please take a chance on me***
> ***By letting me be me***

I can barely see by the end as tears stream down my face. Here I've been so worked up by his silence all day, and he's been busy writing this? God, this is what I get for overthinking everything.

When the song ends, and the crowd calms down from their thunderous appreciation of his performance, the judge, Janet, chimes in with a laugh. "Wow… did you really write that song today?"

Jax nods once as he speaks into the mic. "Yes, I did."

This time James asks, "And is this Sloane in the audience tonight?"

"Yes, sir, she is."

James chuckles. "A lot of girls will be envious of Sloane after that amazing performance."

"Wait..." Janet interrupts. "Are you talking about Sloane Lancaster?"

Holy shit... they're really discussing me—and now my blubbering face is on the freaking jumbotron behind Jax. If I weren't so shocked that he proclaimed he loves me, I'd probably have the sense to be mortified.

"Well..." James chortles. "It looks like she might just feel the same."

"I sure hope so," Jax says without missing a beat. "She means everything to me."

Doing my best to ignore myself being projected behind Jax, through watery eyes, I lock eyes on him and nod in agreement. "I love you, too."

"Well, if that isn't the sweetest thing..." Janet swoons.

Chapter 25
Jax

The moment I walk off stage, I've only got one thing on my mind—I need Sloane. Watching those tears stream down her face as I sang, I wanted so badly to walk off the stage and show her just what she means to me. But of course, I had to follow protocol.

Thankfully, she must feel the same as we somehow meet in the contestant tent. People keep trying to talk to me, but I only have eyes for her. I have a million things I need to say, but the moment I'm close enough to touch her, I pull her in, and my lips meld with hers.

Swiping my tongue along the seam of her lips, it feels like the world is right again. Especially when she opens her mouth, returning my kiss with so much passion. I swear we could probably light this place on fire.

All that matters is being here with her.

Her hands dig into my hair as her body molds against mine. Every ounce of emotion I've tried to convey pours out of me through this kiss.

She. Is. My. Everything.

When we can no longer breathe, we break apart, gasping for air.

For a long moment, I simply rest my forehead to hers as I regain my breath.

"God, I love you, Sloane. You have no idea what you mean to me."

"Uh... I think I might just have an idea," she says on the most beautiful laugh. "You just outed us to the entire world." Running her palm along my stubbled cheek, she swirls her thumb over my swollen lips. "For the record, I love you, too, Jax."

My mind is swirling with a million things, but in this moment, all that matters is that she loves me.

"Please forgive me for being such an ass."

The sweetest laugh escapes her lips. "You're only an ass when you go radio silent. Next time something is wrong—talk to me. We'll work through whatever is bothering you, together."

Kissing her chastely, I promise, "I will. Trust me."

"So..." she draws out, as she runs her finger along my chest. "Did you really write that song *today*?"

Chuckling, I admit, "Yep. It hit me like a ton of bricks and poured out of me all at once. I hope you're not too mad at me for changing up my playlist."

Cocking a brow, she flashes an adorable grin. "Normally—I wouldn't advise such a thing—especially with everything riding on it in this competition."

"That song was the one I needed to sing tonight. I don't care if I win the competition as long as I have my girl."

She shakes her head in amusement. "You're such a fool, Jax Cartwright. But I love you anyway."

"Jax, you're needed on stage!" a deep voice calls out from behind us.

Leaning in, Sloane presses her lips to mine. "I'll love you—no matter what happens out there."

"Good." I kiss her once more. "Because you're stuck with me."

ONCE AGAIN, I'm back on stage, waiting for results. If anyone would've asked me two months ago about this competition, I would've laughed in their face at the thought of entering, let alone being a finalist.

Last time I stood on this stage awaiting results, I was a bumbling ball of nervous energy. This time, my nerves are gone. I'll either win, or I won't. Either way, I'm going on tour, and I'm spending the next six months living the life of a rock star. Dreams I never knew existed are coming true, and I get to do it all with Sloane.

All five of us finalists are spread across the stage, eagerly waiting as the judges make positive comments about each performance. Unlike last time, as they talk about the strengths of each act, they also explain our shortcomings and dismiss us one by one—until it's down to two.

I must give Sloane credit. The final two contestants are the ones she hand-selected to be here. The judges have made it extremely clear that even though she's sought out the talent—she's had nothing to do with the judging aspects of this competition. If we win, it's completely on our own merits. Hopefully, these accolades for Sloane will skyrocket her credibility in the industry.

The judges take their sweet time telling both the members of Edgewater and me what an amazing job we've done. They go back and forth and tell us what'd they'd like to see with us and our careers moving forward.

Eventually, it's time to tell us their decision. As the dramatic music plays—I'll admit—I was lying to myself. My nerves are back with a vengeance as I await the results.

"And the winner of this year's Seaside Music Festival Competition is... Jax... Cartwright!"

Holy fucking shit! I'm officially a rock star!

Epilogue
Raven

My sisters are dropping like flies.

They're falling in love and having the time of their lives.

Don't get me wrong, I'm ecstatic for them. I love seeing them happy.

But I'm not ready for that type of commitment.

I can't even keep a plant alive, let alone find someone worthy of getting past a third date.

As the only sister done with school and single as a pringle, I have to do something fast, or I'll be my matchmaking aunt's next victim.

When Jax's drummer joins him for the summer and needs some help with his image, I make him a deal he can't refuse.

All is perfect—until I realize my summer proposal has one minor flaw.

Our relationship may be a sham, but there's nothing fake about my feelings for Finn.

THE END

THIS MAY BE the end of Sloane and Jax's story in The Summer Ultimatum, but it is not the end of the Lancaster sisters' stories. Find out what happens to Raven and Finn next in The Summer Proposal.

Start Reading Today: https://books2read.com/SummerProposal

You can also see how Ryan and Lanie's story began in The Summer Dare. It is now available, and you can grab your copy today:

https://books2read.com/SummerDare

AUTHOR'S NOTE: If you like reading books set in one world, you'll be happy to find several full-length stories for several of the characters mentioned in The Summer Ultimatum already written and available on my website www.amandashelley.com.

Be sure you stay up to date with all things Amanda Shelley by joining my newsletter: https://geni.us/AmandaShelleyNL

ACKNOWLEDGMENTS

First, I would like to thank you the reader, blogger, and reviewer for taking the time to read this book. There are so many stories to choose from, and I'm humbly honored you've chosen to read mine. I hope you enjoyed Sloane and Jax's story. If you want more from the from their word, be sure to check out the Perfectly Independent Series.

I'd love to hear from you and your thoughts about Sloane and Jax. You can find me on social media, my reader's group *Amanda's Army of Readers*, or at www.amandashelley.com. If you care to share your thoughts on this book with other book lovers, please consider leaving a review at any of the retail sites or on Goodreads, BingeBooks, and BookBub.

I'd like to thank C.L. Collier for being my partner in crime and making the Summer in Seaside Series come to life. She helped make this random thought I had one day, turn into an amazing multi-author collaboration. With her help, we plan to continue this series for years to come.

I'd also like to thank the authors in this series for taking a chance on us as collaborators and taking this journey with us. I couldn't be prouder of what we accomplished together!

This book wouldn't be what it is without my amazing team. First of all, I'd like to thank Mickel Yantz, my supportive beta reader. He's my go-to friend who helps me as I plot, unsticks me from the weeds, and helps me recover the story when things go awry. Thank you for always being willing to listen. Thanks also for your willingness to talk as if my characters and their problems are real. I appreciate your suggestions along the way.

Next I'd like to thank Sue Soares at SJS Editorial Services. You are amazing to work with. I appreciate your patience and flexibility. I simply love working with you. My books wouldn't be what they are without you.

To Julie Deaton at Deaton Author Services, thanks for making my book pretty and talking me off a ledge. I appreciate knowing your proofreading is exquisite, and my worries disappear. I know that if I make you feel all the feels, I've met my mark. Your eagle eyes are spectacular, and I don't know what I'd do without you.

To the people who have supported me along the way, I'm humbly grateful to have you in my life. Whether you've read my books, asked me about my progress, listened to me talk about my fictional characters as if they're a part of my family, plotted with me, or been my cheerleader, I appreciate your continued support. Please know it hasn't gone unnoticed.

Last but certainly not least, to my four beautiful girls who have had to wait patiently when I said, "Just one more minute," when I obviously meant a lot more than one. I love that you get that I have deadlines and will sometimes keep me on task with your not-so-subtle reminders that "Mom... you should be working" during my designated times. I appreciate your support more than you'll ever know. Even though you can't read this book—because that might be *weird*—for both of us, I love that you keep asking. I love you all more than words can express. You're the reason I continue to strive and reach for my goals each day.

ABOUT THE AUTHOR

Amanda Shelley writes romantic stories you can escape into. Some are steamy, others are sweet but all have strong characters with a little bit of sass.

When not writing, Amanda enjoys time with her family, playing chauffeur, chef and being an enthusiastic fan for her children. Keeping up with them keeps her alert and grounded in reality. She enjoys long car rides, chai lattes and popping her SUV into four-wheel drive for adventures anywhere.

Amanda loves hearing from readers. Be sure to sign up for her newsletter and follow her on social media. Join her reader's group Amanda's Army of Readers to stay up to date on her latest information.

Readers group:
https://www.facebook.com/groups/AmandasArmyofReaders/
Goodreads:
https://www.goodreads.com/author/show/19713563.Amanda_Shelley
Newsletter:
https://geni.us/AmandaShelleyNL
www.amandashelley.com
Website:
www.amandashelley.com

Facebook:
https://www.facebook.com/authoramandashelley/
Instagram:
https://www.instagram.com/authoramandashelley/
Twitter:
https://twitter.com/AmandShelley
Tik Tok:
https://www.tiktok.com/@authoramandashelley
Amazon:
https://www.amazon.com/author/amandashelley
Book Bub:
https://www.bookbub.com/profile/amanda-shelley

ALSO BY AMANDA SHELLEY

If you enjoyed this book, you will be happy to discover Amanda Shelley primarily writes in one world. For a complete list of the series reading order as well as a chronological time line, please visit:

https://amandashelley.com/reading-order/

The Summer Dare:

Leave it to Nana to think of everything.

After a grueling semester, I'm ready for a peaceful summer in Seaside with my sisters.

Imagine my surprise, when I'm woken by the screeching sound of a saw coming through my wall, the first official morning of break.

Not only did I come flying out of bed swinging, but I gave Ryan, the unsuspecting carpenter the surprise of his life, when I came wielding my killer coat hanger and all.

Too bad, I was only in a tank and undies and it wasn't nearly as effective as I'd hoped.

Of course, he insists he's only doing his job. Since it's Nana's last request to care for us, I can't refuse.

However, I won't let a tall, pesky, sexy as sin, know-it-all get in my way of my summer plans. I pretend I ignore him - that is until my youngest sister pokes her nose in my business and throws down a dare I can't back down from.

Kiss the next single guy who walks up to the bonfire - or explain to my sisters why I get riled up over the contractor.

When Ryan suddenly appears, I know I'm screwed in more ways than one.

Not only will my sisters learn my secret, but from the determined look on Ryan's face, I'm afraid he's eager to reveal it to the world as well.

What have I gotten myself into?

As I walk toward him, one thing is certain - *this summer dare will either make or break me.*

https://geni.us/AmandaShelleyBooks

The Summer Proposal

My sisters are dropping like flies.

They're falling in love and having the time of their lives.

Don't get me wrong, I'm ecstatic for them. I love seeing them happy.

But I'm not ready for that type of commitment.

I can't even keep a plant alive, let alone find someone worthy of getting past a third date.

As the only sister done with school and single as a pringle, I have to do something fast, or I'll be my matchmaking aunt's next victim.

When Jax's drummer joins him for the summer and needs some help with his image, I make him a deal he can't refuse.

All is perfect—until I realize my summer proposal has one minor flaw.

Our relationship may be a sham, but there's nothing fake about my feelings for Finn.

https://geni.us/AmandaShelleyBooks

The Summer Arrangement

One, two, three—it's all down to me.

As the youngest and only single Lancaster, I'm eager to spend my summer in Seaside, Oregon, with my sisters. It's something I've looked forward to all year, and I'm determined to make every minute count. After all, I've only got one year before I graduate from college and have to adult for real.

However, if I want to graduate debt free, I need to work. I have a lead on the perfect summer job with the nanny agency I've spent the last three summers catering to.

I just have to win over an adorable three-year-old and convince her single dad I'm the right one for the job.

Simple enough, right?

Except when I show up at his door, I'm shocked to find he's the guy I hooked up with a few times last semester.

This cannot be happening.

I need this job. There's too much on the line to walk away. Maybe we can put the past behind us and make some sort of summer arrangement?

https://geni.us/AmandaShelleyBooks

The Summer I Found Home

Being a pilot is all I've ever known.

I served my country and I'm damn proud of my career.

But sacrifices were made, especially when it came to family.

I've missed first steps, first days of school, and first dates to name a few.

My kids grew up. They're having families of their own.

Was it worth it?

When an opportunity brings me to Seaside, I jump feet first no questions asked.

It means experiencing all those firsts with my grandkids.

With family as my focus and my guard down, I don't even see Faye coming.

She's a force to be reckoned with and has me holding on for dear life.

I thought our ship had sailed, but now that I'm home for good—I just might get more than one second chance.

arrangement?

https://geni.us/AmandaShelleyBooks

Zander: A Perfectly Independent Series Novella

(Available for free on All Retailers)

Zander's known for being a player both on and off the court. When his name shows up as my next client, my heart stalls, and not in a good way. There's no way I'll survive the semester with him. I just don't have the patience.

However, when I need help, Zander makes a proposal I can't refuse. He'll be my fake date to my best friend's wedding so I don't have to face my ex and his new girlfriend alone.

The weekend goes off without a hitch as we effortlessly pretend to have the time of our lives.

All is perfect... until I realize my feelings for Zander are no longer an act.

What will I do when our arrangement comes to an end?

https://geni.us/AmandaShelleyBooks

Drew: Book One of the Perfectly Independent Series

Of all people, why him?

He didn't EVEN bother introducing himself, just assumed I knew him from his fame on the court.

I nearly died on the spot when our professor announced we were permanent lab partners. Between his arrogance and the constant interruption from basketball groupies, there's no way I'll survive this semester.

Sure, he's hotter than anyone I've ever seen in a science lab with his sexy blue eyes, cute dimple, and muscles for days - but I can't afford *his* kind of distractions.

Okay. Deep breath.

I can do this.

After all, it's only one semester.

Just when I think my self-control is in check, he does something to show me that he isn't the egotistical, self-centered jerk I thought he was.

How can his stupid smile suddenly make my mind melt, heart race, and palms sweat?

If I take this chance on Drew, will my perfectly laid out plans disappear?

Vince: Book Two of the Perfectly Independent Series

It's funny how one night can change everything.

As a bartender near campus, I'm certain I've heard it all. Rarely a shift passes without some guy taking his best shot, hoping I'll end my self-proclaimed dating diet.

Of course, this is exactly how I meet Vince.

Except, he isn't the one running his mouth.

No, he simply shuts down his idiotic friend, then stops my heart with the simplest of smiles and walks away.

Just when I force myself to forget him, he bumps into me on campus.

Our connection is consuming, and my world is knocked off kilter. It's far beyond physical attraction. He's smart, sexy, and feels like—home?

Wait, that can't be right...

Whatever it is, Vince has me breaking my rules to spend time with him.

My entire life I've prepared for meeting the wrong guys.

Damien: Book Three of the Perfectly Independent Series

Beautiful girls are not hard to find at Columbia River University.

The coeds on campus are great to look at but I was over that scene after graduation three years ago.

These days, outside of being part of the largest civil engineering job on campus, all I'm searching for is a decent meal and some peace and quiet. It's why I'm happy to have found what I consider a hidden gem in the diner I frequent.

All I need to do is finish this job and move on to the next by year's end.

Should be easy enough. Only when Vanessa walks up with a sexy smile and a mouth full of sass, she does more than take my order. She completely takes my breath away.

Next thing I know, I'm here every morning, making every excuse to dine with this intriguing woman. Not only is she smart and sexy, but she's laser focused on reaching the goals she's set for herself.

The more I get to know her, the more I'm convinced she's the one. I just have to find a way to get her to deviate from her perfectly laid plans and take a chance on me.

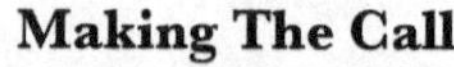

https://geni.us/AmandaShelleyBooks

Making The Call

Dani

As a bestselling romance author, most assume my life's glamorous, filled with combustible chemistry, and most of all, romance. Ha! I can only wish. With a deadline looming, I've escaped to my family's cabin on Anderson Island to free myself from distractions. My plan's great, until a man, who could pass as a cover model on one of my books, comes to my rescue. Is there chemistry? Sure. Is he everything I'd look for in a guy? Absolutely. But will my career be at risk if I give into my desire?

Luke

For a player, women line up outside the locker room. For coaches, we're lucky to get in the game. As the youngest NFL coach in the league, I live, eat, breathe, and even sleep football. To gear up for this season, I return to my home on Anderson Island for a much-needed break. When Dani literally crashes into my life, my mind's suddenly on the sexy brunette with a sailors mouth, rather than my team's next play. She has me dusting off another playbook entirely, making me wonder, did I make the right call?

https://geni.us/AmandaShelleyBooks

The Boy Upstairs

I ran into Derek while trying to escape the neighbor from hell.

Instantly, we hit it off. Since he's only here for three months and the microbrewery leaves me little time for commitments, it's the perfect setup for a fling.

He's adventurous, challenges me, and he just gets me from the inside out.

With our expiration date quickly approaching, I'm left to wonder...
Will my heart ever be the same without the boy upstairs?

https://geni.us/AmandaShelleyBooks

He Saved My Boy

Davis is the first guy to catch my attention since... hell, I don't even know.

Instantly, he makes me think and feel things I've forgotten existed. It has been forever since I put my needs first, so I take the chance and let him light me up from the inside out.

Our night is the kind that will ruin me for all others.

But then I get the dreaded call.

I rush out without a second glance, knowing I'll likely never see him again.

My son will always come first—Always.

Imagine my surprise when Davis walks in, and I find he's the only one who can save my boy.

This cannot be happening—*I guess it's time to pull up my big girl panties and see what happens.*

https://geni.us/AmandaShelleyBooks

---

not only won the campaign, but I'm apparently married to the man I've only ever let myself fantasize about.

The kicker of it all – he has no intentions of letting me go.

But what will it mean once we leave Vegas?

https://geni.us/AmandaShelleyBooks

Resilience: Book One of Resilience Duet

Resolution: Book Two of Resilience Duet

Samantha never saw Enzo coming.

As the dust settles from her divorce, her life is full. She doesn't have time for distractions. She's too busy running her own company and checking off numerous items from her kids' demanding schedule to have a life of her own.

Then he walks into her kitchen with his breathtaking green eyes and a mischievous grin. He's there to surprise his father - her contractor, but his presence makes everything off kilter.

Enzo's perfectly content with his adventurous life as an elite rescue pilot, until a harmless prank turns on him. Instead of surprising his father, he finds his world thrown off course by the beautiful woman with a sexy smile, wicked sass and the mouthwatering ability to keep him on his toes.

With his limited time on leave, is she worth the risk to his heart?

https://geni.us/AmandaShelleyBooks

Collide: A Sweet Romance

Falling head over heels was the last thing I expected.

Literally.

Coffee is everywhere – and more than my ego is bruised.

When the handsome stranger I plowed into calls me by name, mortification sinks in.

He rushes off to class. I run home to change, hoping to forget the whole incident.

If only I could be so lucky.

I quickly find it's a small world and Gavin Wallace is completely unavoidable. Everywhere I turn he's there. In my classes. Hanging with my friends.

I've got his full attention and I have to admit, I like it a lot more than I should.

https://geni.us/AmandaShelleyBooks